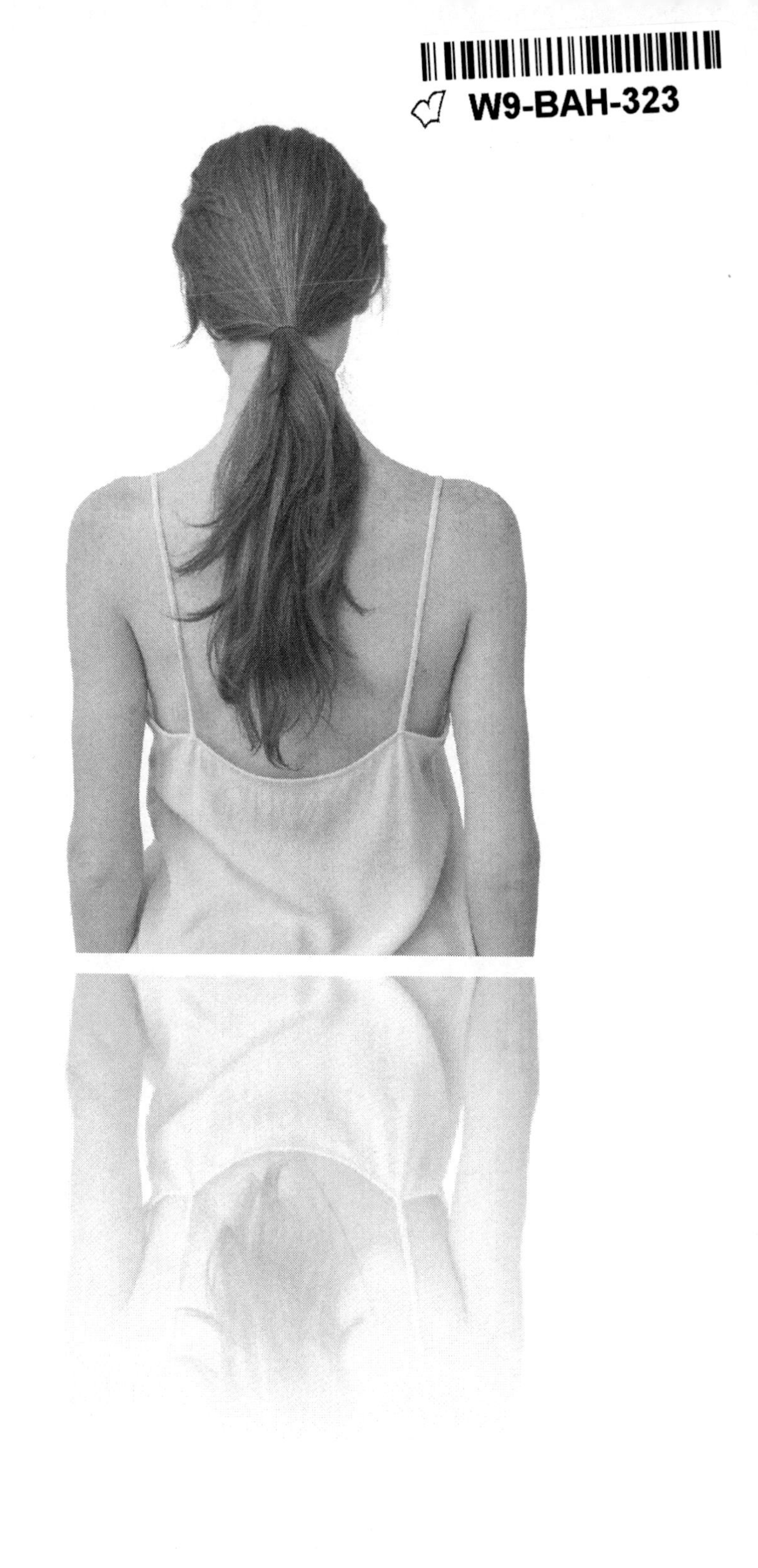

#heartmatch

A novella by

C.K. Alber

#heartmatch

Published by C.K. Alber, 2018

Print Edition

Edited by Lori Corsentino

Cover Design by © Lori Corsentino/Harmony Creative Design

Image: Slay19, Cookiestudio/Bigstock Photo

C.K. Alber

Visit my website at www.ckalber.com

Printed in the United States of America

First Edition: June, 2018, C.K. Alber

ISBN: 978-1-9832008-5-4

"Let's exchange numbers," he typed.

One minute later, Samantha's phone rang. She answered the Facetime call.

"Hey, nothing's ugly so far," Jason said.

She moved her phone around the room. "This is where I live."

"In a bedroom?" he asked.

"A hospital room."

His brows furrowed.

"What happened? You have an accident?"

"I'm dying, Jason."

She moved the phone to her IV, the heart monitor machine, her face.

Her voice trembled with emotion. "If I want to live, someone dies."

"I don't get it." His stare sharpened. His gray eyes darkened. "Sam, I mean ah—" he paused. "I'm not feeling too well. I gotta go."

Jason disconnected.

Contents

Dedication

A special dedication to my daughters—Jeanie Marie, Cynthia Ann, and Donna Caterina. All I ever hope to be, I owe to the greatest three mothers of all.

I also want to thank four teens close to my heart. Thank you—Trevor, Nikolas, Jack, and Andrew for helping me with the main character in this book. Your suggestions and comments helped a lot.

FEBRUARY 1

Wednesday

The late morning sun glistened off freshly fallen flakes. The last Rocky Mountain winter storm had settled over the landscape. Even with a recently lit fire crackling in the bedroom fireplace, a chill engulfed Samantha Brown's body. She stared out the window, glimpsing the artistic Christmas card scene from her usual extended position on her bed.

The carefully stitched, colorful quilt her mother had made years before, decorated with photos depicting some of her favorite childhood memories, covered her, lending warmth. She wiggled her toes. Fluffy bright-pink socks peeked from under the cover. Her new laptop lay across her thighs, lid open. She tapped the keys again.

Why isn't he answering me today?

Samantha had at last found an online friend. Jason's profile picture displayed a young man, royal-blue kerchief covering most of his head. Shoots of dark, curly hair poked from beneath the colorful fabric. Luscious gray eyes, the color of ash, stared into the camera. Light brown skin. A prominent cleft chin below an unsmiling mouth.

A gentle tap sounded at the door. Samantha closed the lid of her computer.

Her beautiful mother, looking older than her forty-five years, breezed into the room and whirled around the bed.

"Leave the curtains open, mother."

Her mother complied and returned to the side of the bed near the desk. "I'll take that, dear."

She lifted the laptop from Samantha's legs and set the computer onto her white desk. Samantha had salvaged the distressed piece from a thrift shop, then stripped and painted the wood white, finishing the project before the fatigue and pain she now endured had begun to ravage her body.

"Probably needs to charge. Don't you think?"

Samantha turned her head to the window and shut out her mother's chatter. Although she was eighteen, her parents handled her like the fluffy flakes that had accumulated outside on the window sill. *Delicately*. Sometimes Samantha had the urge to run away from the clutches of her illness.

But that will never happen.

Loneliness overcame Samantha. Most of her friends had abandoned her two years ago when she'd become home-prisoned. She had a million things she wanted to talk about that no parent would understand. With no one to share her thoughts, she combed the web for someone to chat with. She needed a connection. Someone who would understand and possibly sympathize.

In bunny house shoes, her mother shuffled over and rested a hand on Samantha's head. She pet her as if Samantha were a cat and then ran fingers through her strawberry-blond tresses, releasing tangles from the night before.

"Ouch. Just brush it."

Her mother sat down on the edge of the bed and rested the same hand that had stroked Samantha's sensitive scalp on her leg.

"Dear, I have something to tell you."

The agonized expression her mother held frightened Samantha.

"Did something happen to daddy?"

"No, my precious. He's fine. Still stuck at a meeting in Seattle."

"Then why the frown?"

"Doctor Sadana's office called this morning." She hesitated. Cleared her throat. "There's a bed for you at the University hospital and—"

"No—please." Samantha wound her fingers tightly together. "No more hospitals. Please."

Three surgical procedures as an infant, other operations as she grew older, pacemakers, radio frequency ablations, incisions, pokes, and needle jabs, all because of a congenital heart defect.

I can't take any more.

"What for this time?" Her voice quivered as a wave of terror washed over her.

A concerned reaction skittered across her mother's face. "Dear, now don't get agitated. It's not good for you."

"Tell me." Blood rushed to her head, throbbing at her temples. "What's happening next?"

"Doctor Sadana says you're a good candidate for a heart transplant."

Samantha glanced toward the window. She closed her eyes and imagined a balmy beach under a warm California sun. Palm trees blew in the wind. She lay on a towel soaking up the rays.

Returning her gaze to her mother, a mere breath erupted from her lips. Samantha whispered. "When?"

"The ambulance will come for you today."

"There's a donor?"

"Not yet. Doctor Sadana has advised us your heart condition can no longer be improved by medication. You're growing weaker."

"Why can't I wait here?"

"Once a donor heart is found, there will only be a short amount of time before the transplantation takes place. He wants you there and ready when that moment arrives."

Samantha covered her mouth with the palm of her hand. She'd read the booklets Doctor Sadana had given her about transplantation. Now reality and the information embedded in her brain about what she'd read scared her. Fear of dying under the scalpel terrorized Samantha. If she mentioned that notion to her mother, she knew she'd only hear the "not to worry" phrase her mother kept repeating.

"A computer generates a match run." Her mother inhaled deeply before continuing. "Blood types, age, weight, height will all be taken into consideration and—"

"Stop!" Samantha put her hands to her ears. "I don't want to hear anymore."

Her mother jumped at the outburst. "You'll have time for a nap before I have to get you ready, dear." She lightly patted her leg. "Not to worry, my precious."

"Just go away. I'm not going anywhere, today or ever."

Samantha returned to her imaginary beach scene. She wanted to stand in the waves, smell the salt water, and watch the seagulls swoop.

Her mother laid a hand on her shoulder, bringing her back to reality. “Could I help you into the bathroom before you rest?”

Samantha glanced down at the quilt and spotted the photo where she’d lost her first tooth and another picture of her riding on her dad’s shoulders as she reached for the clouds.

Has my life ever been normal?

“No,” she uttered with annoyance. “Not going.”

Her mother gulped, holding back a sob.

“Give me my computer.”

“You should have a break from technology, sweetheart. A nap would be more beneficial than—”

“No, I need to check something. Please.” She attempted to sweet-talk her mother.

“I could bring in the pamphlets Doctor Sadana gave you to read,” her mother offered. “Reading is easier on the mind and could lull you to sleep.”

“I want to do a Google search,” she lied.

Her mother’s head bobbed. “Okay. Thirty minutes and I’ll be back in.” She retrieved the laptop and placed the device across Samantha’s legs.

Her mother sighed before scooting around the bed once again. She picked up Samantha's cell phone. "Battery charged and good to go. Text me if you need anything." She laid the cell on the nightstand and floated back over to the door then stopped and stared long and hard at her.

Samantha exhaled, blowing out a puff of air between parched lips as she returned her mother's gaze. "You aren't going to cry, are you?"

Her mother's posture straightened. "No, my child. Not today."

She left, closing the door softly behind her.

Samantha went to the #heartmatch site and tapped in a message.

"You there?"

No answer.

"I need to ask a question. Please answer."

As she waited, she wondered if she'd be able to take her computer to the hospital. She hoped so.

Ding.

Jason's profile picture popped up. *"You woke me up."*

"Sorry."

"What you want, kid?"

"I'm not a kid." She included a mad emoji.

"Scrap the crap. I'm outta here."

Think of something to keep him interested. Hurry. Brain-wracking time.

"Hey!!!!!!" Jason tapped. *"Said I'm leavin."*

"*Would you ever kill a woman?*" Samantha hit the worried emoji key.

"In the games? Why not?"

"In real life?" She tapped the broken heart emoji, then wished she hadn't.

"You crazy? What's with the jagged heart?"

"Someone might die and I'll play a part in their death."

"You joking me?"

"I have to go." She disconnected, knowing she'd said too much.

Samantha touched the bedspread photo of a trip to the mountains she'd taken with her parents.

Snow angels flitted across her mind. The sensation of falling snow on her tongue and the tingling of the tips of her fingers and toes from the cold.

Why these memories? The past and happier times maybe. Live in the present, her dad always said.

"It's not about tomorrow. It's all about now," she said, parroting his words.

She rested her head on the pillow.

Somewhere in the state of Colorado, a kid named Jason lived. From what Samantha could decipher from the brief conversations between them, they had nothing in common.

I like him, but he wouldn't understand this.

Her hand waved over the bed, then around the room. She heard a noise coming from the hall and pretended to sleep as her mother tiptoed in to retrieve her computer.

FEBRUARY 5

Sunday

Jason Bryant's fingers drummed the top of his desk as he continued his long, nerve-wracking wait. The wind whistled through a crack in the window frame. A streetlamp outside, now almost obliterated by blowing snow, usually gave light enough for him to see when his mom's silver four-wheel-drive pulled in the driveway of their tri-level house.

Every damn time she worked the night shift his gut churned with worry. He jumped to his feet, wincing as the chair toppled and crashed to the floor. He ran to the bathroom, flung open the door, fell to his knees over the toilet, and spewed the nachos he'd snacked on hours before. A few minutes later, Jason's hand lifted to the handle and flushed the ugly evidence down with the swirling water.

Where the hell is she?

He pulled a hand towel off the rack, wiped his chin, and tossed the moistened cloth to the pile of dirty clothes in the corner.

His reflection in the mirror netted his attention. Jason stood ramrod straight. Brows furrowed. The stubble of a beard and a riot of dark curls coiled in every direction. He inspected his teeth, opened his mouth wide, and did the side view stance.

Damn.

The only difference between him and his forty-nine-year-old double were his gray eyes, the color of lint in the dryer tray. The man who had abandoned him had eyes the color of charcoal.

“Frickin bastard.”

He picked up the soap dish and flung the ceramic swan at the mirror. Shards of glass fell into the sink and onto the floor. Jason treaded around the fragments, then left the scene and returned to the hallway.

The pocket of his sweat pants vibrated. He pulled the cell phone out from the depths and read.

“On way.”

“Shit.” He raced to his bedroom and glared out the window examining the street as far as he could see. No car lights. Nothing.

"Who the hell goes out in the middle of the night when the weather's like this? Can't see a damn thing."

Jason knew about his mom's secret indulgence and for that reason his heart raced with worry. He also knew her speed would be calculatingly slow, white knuckled hands gripping the steering wheel as she made the trip home to him and the security of their house.

"Mom, stay safe," he tapped on his phone keys.

Jason turned around to the familiar surroundings of his room. Sonic, the dog he found in a fast food parking lot, lay at the foot of his bed. Sports posters lined one wall. A colorful blanket his grandma had crocheted lay over the back of an arm chair. A flat screen television above a chest-of-drawers. Simple. The way he liked things.

His gaze shifted to the back of his computer.

Ding. Ding.

Jason picked up the fallen chair and dropped onto its wicker seat, sitting in front of the screen. He craved his bong. *Weed.* His kind of smoke.

No smoking inside. His mom's rules.

He stared at the screen.

"How old are you?" Along with a smiley emoji.

Jason's fingers flew over the keys as he typed a message. *"Nineteen. Told you the first time."*

"You said you graduated. Did you fail a year?" Sad face emoji pops up.

"I finished last year."

"Are you in college?" Smiley face emoji.

"No."

Jason hardly knew this girl. Her questions irritated him. He hated having to answer questions. To anyone. His anxiousness about his mom's whereabouts redirected to his computer conversation. He threw his hands up in the air aiming both middle fingers at the screen. He should close the lid and stop this immature shit. Instead, something kept him connected.

He pressed shift and the exclamation point key. *"!!!!!"* He refused to bring up one emoji.

"What's that mean?" She typed.

He loathed nosey people. This girl Samantha had searched him out. Not the other way around–and she chose to put a cartoon character's photo as her profile picture. Jason stared at the screen. "She calls herself Buttercup? You gotta be kidding me."

His computer dinged, jerking his attention back to the cartoon character in front of him.

"Hey. You there?"

"Yep." His stare lifted to the window, then to his watch. His stomach turned.

Ding.

"Do you ever sleep?" Smiley face.

He pressed Star on his phone. The call went straight to his mom's voicemail. Her soft-spoken automatic response did nothing to ease his worry.

Can't she ever remember to call me at a stop light?

No because his mom worried he'd be asleep at this hour and didn't want to wake him. He'd never tell her he could only sleep after she'd arrived back from work and walked through the front door. Jason always had a lingering fear one day something bad would happen to her. No, he couldn't sleep, especially during these ice-covered, snow-packed street days when his mom had to drive.

Ding.

"Hey, you there?"

He avoided Samantha's question and glanced at his watch again. His glare flew back to the window as a car passed, traveling cautiously down the slippery street. Jason jumped up, rushed to the glass, and craned his neck trying to see beyond the gusting snow. He fidgeted with the curtain tie. Sonic whined.

Ding. Ding.

Jason edged back to the screen. A bitter taste rose and fell in the back of his throat.

Ten more minutes before I go outside to search.

He plopped down, pausing for a moment before tapping the keys. *"You still here?"*

"Hey. That's mean." Pouty emoji appeared.

The image of the Buttercup cartoon with non-blinking eyes stared at him. *"It's after five. I'm signing out."*

"Wait."

"?" He typed in a question mark.

"My parents don't want me online. Predators they say. So, when my mother and dad go to sleep, I get connected."

"So? What's that got to do with me?" His gaze lifted. Jason wanted to run outside and trot down a block or two. Maybe she'd slid into a ditch and needed help.

Ding.

"You play those frightful gun games?" Emoji with wide eyes flashed on the screen.

"Jeez," he said under his breath even though the girl couldn't hear him.

"I've played a game or two." Samantha tapped in a Smiley face with halo.

His curiosity piqued. For a moment he forgot why his attention span was zero. *"Oh?"*

"Yah. I especially like the one where they use the club."

"And the spade too?" He smirked as he thought about the card game his grandma played by herself online. *"Games for the bored."*

"Oh, this one does everything but bore me."

"I'm not impressed."

Another smiley face and an emoji with horns. *"I shot a guy."*

Headlights glared, lighting up his room as a car moved into the driveway.

Mom.

Jason turned back to the computer.

"You killed someone dead?"

"Yep. I recently got this new computer. I've been experimenting."

"With games?"

"Games, research, chat rooms. Hashtag Heart Match where I found you."

A car door slammed.

"I was surfing some sites when you stumbled onto me," Jason explained.

"And your name accidently got typed in?" Smiley face.

"Jeez. Will you cut the crap with the fricking emojis?"

The front door opened.

"Hey." Sad face emoji popped up.

Door slammed.

"Jase, you awake? Your light's on."

A pause. He could picture his mom slipping off her coat and hanging the fake fur jacket on the tall wooden post. Next, she'd probably toe off her ankle boots.

"Sweetheart? Are you still up?"

His bedroom door stood wide open. He powered off and closed the laptop lid.

"Five, four, three, two, one," he said under his breath, then jumped up and pivoted around.

"There you are." His mom stood in the door frame. She strode over and encased him in a bear hug. "Are you looking at colleges?"

He nodded. "Yup."

"Anyplace I know?" she asked hopefully.

"Been talkin' to Sam." His chin jutted toward his desk. "Don't know more than that."

His mom squeezed him tighter. "A new friend. That's nice. I'll fix you some bacon and eggs," she whispered.

Seconds later she let go and held him at arm's length. She then tilted and hiccupped.

Shit. Damned vodka.

A smile lifted the corners of her mouth. "My adorable son. You waited up for me. What would I do without you?"

That's what she usually said. He always answered the same thing.

"You'd find someone who deserves you and get married again."

His mom's head bobbed. She grabbed his hand and pulled him from the room.

"And what would you do if I remarried?"

Jason shrugged. "How about French toast today?"

He grasped her shoulders from behind and with a gentle shove, directed her towards her bedroom. "Go shower, mom. Breakfast in fifteen minutes."

"Okay," she said sleepily as she weaved her way down the hallway, bracing herself along the walls for support.

The shower ran as he cooked. Jason poured orange juice into long-stemmed goblets, made a fresh pot of coffee, and flipped the bread in the iron skillet.

The shower water turned off. He'd be lucky if his mom came to the table. She'd worked her usual all-night shift at the hospital emergency room. On her drive home, she'd probably emptied her sleep aid from the flask she hid in her bag. No conversation with her lasted very long when she drank. He'd give anything to have his dad here. There'd been no word from him since he'd left with that young bitch and headed west.

Bastard.

He pulled the kitchen curtain aside. The snow continued to fall. Icicles hung from the garage roof. Jason could breathe easy now.

She's home and safe.

He cocked his head to listen. No sounds indicated she would join him in the kitchen.

The heater kicked on and blew out air, making the house more cozy and warm. His mom would sleep under a mound of covers until late afternoon. At least she was home now and under his watchful eye. She worked long hours so she could pay the bills, keep the house in her name, and take care of him. Jason never complained about the alcohol she downed every day, but her vodka consumption gnawed inwardly at him.

He glanced at the clock over the stove. In a couple of hours grandma would do her unannounced pop in, bringing with her a warm lunch in a basket. Jason forked a slice of his breakfast from the pan, plopped down on a stiff wooden chair at the table, poured syrup, and ate. After he downed the last of his juice, he rose and carried the few dishes to the sink.

He tiptoed down the hallway to the master bedroom. He lingered in the doorway, assessing the scene before him. Empty glass on the nightstand next to his mom's cell phone. Towel dropped to the wooden floor, along with a nightgown.

He edged over to the bed and watched the rise and fall of the covers. A slight snore erupted as she changed her position under the comforter from side to back. Damp red hair lay splashed across the pillow. Below her earlobe, on her neck, he saw the tick of her heartbeat.

Where's the bottle?

Jason bent over to look under the bed. There lay an empty glass container, a sure sign his mom had guzzled the contents dry.

Another day, another bottle.

His parent's black and white wedding picture, in a decorative silver frame, stood on her dresser. His grandma talked about how, in the eighties, their contrasting skin colors tore his family apart. Regardless, his parents had remained together through it all until this previous year. Jason got the news about their divorce the day after he graduated from high school. He'd been shattered as he watched his dad leave, car loaded to the hilt, on his way to California.

"Come with me" his dad had yelled after pulling away from the driveway. Jason shook his head. "Your loss" his dad shouted then waved from the sunroof as he shot down the street, leaving everyone who loved him behind.

Jason had fallen to his knees and sobbed. Afterward, he had gone inside to the bathroom and spent the entire night with his head in the bowels of the toilet, vomiting his guts out.

No matter what happened, Jason would never leave his mom. The day his dad left had destroyed his mom's lust for life. The world he knew changed. No more family vacations. No more friends. No college. Nothing. That's when he'd taken up blood and guts computer games.

"Yeah, crap on 'til death do us part," he mumbled.

With the empty bottle under his arm, Jason headed to his room and the games he'd come to rely on to purge his anger. He'd trash the empty bottle sometime before his grandma came to check on them. Now he had to kill someone on the screen and vent his animosity for those in the orbit of this world he hated.

FEBRUARY 6

Monday

"What kind of tea you makin?" Jason flipped two burgers in an iron skillet before he turned from the stove to face his mom.

He watched as she ran fingers through her coppery curls and raised her gaze to his. Her hazel eyes sparkled as a smile lifted the corners of her mouth.

"Since when do you care about what I'm drinking?"

"I pay attention to everything you do."

If you only knew.

He turned around to take the hamburgers out of the pan with a spatula, put them in buns, and load their plates with fries fresh from the oven. He placed the dishes on the table and plopped down in the chair opposite his mom.

He pointed a fry at the china cup. "Mint?" And then bit into the potato.

"Chamomile."

She turned her head but not before he saw a tinge of color on her cheeks.

His mom bit into the burger, chewed, then turned back to search Jason's face.

"Have you heard from your dad?"

Jason shook his head before pouring ketchup over his fries.

"Why don't you call him?" She took another bite.

"Now why would I wanna to do that?" Jason never answered his dad's incessant texts or phone calls.

The bastard.

"Jason, look." She took in a deep breath and slowly expelled the air. "He's not coming back. He chose to start over someplace else with another person."

He studied her. Even though she'd said the words, she didn't sound like she was totally convinced herself.

"You can't go on hating him for that choice."

Oh yes, I can.

"We loved each other to the end, at least until our roads separated." She pushed her meal away. "He went his way and I went mine."

A sob caught in her throat, confirming she still had pain. So did he. They dealt with their pain in different ways. Jason chose to lock himself in his room and play violent games to forget about his fricking dad, while his mom drank herself into oblivion. Right now, she appeared halfway rational. Four hours from now she'd be unsteady on her feet.

Because of these changes, Dad will forever be a damned bastard, at least in my mind.

"Now let's talk about what's next for you." She rested her elbow on the table and cradled her cheek in her open hand.

His gut twisted. Jason wanted to avoid the speech he got every other day. Sonic whined, probably from the rise in tension. Jason rose to let him out and then lit the fire under the tea kettle, avoiding her glare.

"Either you go back to school or you get a job."

He turned at her sharp tone just as she got up, clutching the lapels to close her robe.

"You can't stay on your computer all night long and sleep all day." Her eyes caught his. "And all of that other stuff young men like you do."

And smoke weed, look at porn, and call sex chat.

The kettle whistled.

Jason picked up his mom's cup and returned to the sink. "I'll add some water to this bag."

With his back to her, he sipped. According to his research, his mom had chosen wisely.

Vodka—the colorless, tasteless, odorless drink.

He swirled the few drops around in his mouth.

Not tastin' like straight tea.

When he turned to comment, his mom's expression chilled him to the bone. One he'd seen before. A ghostly, fragile look that could easily crumble into pieces. The same countenance as the day his dad had abandoned them.

Yeah, mom. I know.

A knock at the back door interrupted their unspoken conversation. The door opened. Sonic came in, followed by Jason's grandma Rosie.

She took in their stances before speaking. "Did I interrupt something?" She didn't wait for an answer as she put the large pot she carried onto the stove. "Ham and beans. Make sure you eat Elizabeth." She commented, scanning his mom's thin body. "You'll blow away if you get any thinner. And you Jason," she enveloped him in chubby arms, "can add all the hot sauce you want. It's home-cooked. Do I get a thank you?" His grandma stared at his mom.

"I've eaten. I'm going to shower."

Grandma glanced at the table. "You already ate lunch? Okay, my next choice. We'll all sit down at the table for dinner before you leave for work, Elizabeth."

"I might not be hungry—"

"We need to talk," grandma interrupted his mom.

"About what?" His mom frowned.

"What's going to happen next in this household."

"We're stayin' here, right mom?" Jason looked from one to the other. Before his dad disappeared, his mom and grandma had a liking for each other. Not so much now.

Jason watched as his mom, hands on hips, took a defiant stance and glared at her mother-in-law. "I pay my bills and I own this house. There's nothing to discuss."

"I have a few things I'd like to say. Afterwards, you can tell me to get lost or not."

"Okay. What you say usually goes anyway. We'll eat together." A flicker of sorrow crossed his mom's eyes before she turned and darted out of the kitchen.

"I have to do some computer work," Jason commented before he hurried away from his grandma and down the same hallway as his mom.

"Wait, mom."

She stopped, although she didn't turn.

Even though Jason knew his mom would consume alcohol before leaving for work, he didn't want her to get sad all over again. Grandma could be a toughie when she wanted. "Just wanted to tell you I love you."

Her head bobbed in acknowledgement before she turned to her room. He heard the door lock turn.

Jason's phone vibrated. He pulled the cell from his pocket and glared at the name that appeared on the screen. "Go to hell, dad," he muttered. He shoved the unanswered phone back into his sweats.

His phone double-dinged. His dad had left a message.

Jason closed and locked his bedroom door before dropping on the chair behind his computer. The vacuum sounded in the distance.

Grandma.

He opened the lid. Checked into the #heartmatch site. "What the heck did Sam mean yesterday? Kill a woman?"

Sam wasn't online.

Jason tapped in a message. *"Where'd you go, Sam? Get back to me."*

He pulled out his phone, took a smiling selfie, plugged the cell into his computer, changed his profile picture, and logged out.

###

At the dinner table, several hours later, grandma shook a fork at both of them as they ate, talking about how good things had been when grandpa was alive and how everything functioned when Matthew had lived in this house.

His mom interrupted her. “Your son is the one who left. There’s nothing more to say.”

“True. That doesn’t mean your life has to be over.” She caught Jason’s eye then turned to his mom. “You both act as if there’s been a death in the family.”

“Well you know what?” His mom got up so fast, the chair tipped over. “That’s the way the breakup feels to me.” She turned the radio on and covered her ears.

“Grandpa died. He’s never coming back. And Mathew—he’s going through the change of life. If he’s smart he’ll realize he’s wrong and come begging,” grandma bellowed over the music.

“And maybe I don’t want him back anymore,” his mom yelled, turning the knob even higher and then humming to shut out any probable response.

“Hey, you two.” Jason hit the button on the radio, turning the machine off. He heaved a deep breath. “Can you stop the bickering and yelling?”

“I’m done here,” his mom left the kitchen and went back to her bedroom.

###

The smell of ham and apple pie hung in the air as his grandma readied to leave. She’d cleaned the house, done the laundry, packed up her dishes, and slipped into her long wool coat. Darkness engulfed Sonic as he ran out the open back door into the fenced-in yard. Jason flipped on the flood lights, waved to his grandma and yelled to her not to slip and fall as he closed the door.

Jason’s mom stood in the hall doorway, dressed in her green scrubs, ready for her night shift at the hospital. She had puffy, bloodshot eyes. Hair sprigs stuck out from a carelessly made braid.

“You leavin?” Jason stepped up to hug her.

She backed away. “Are you siding with grandma?”

“Mom,” Jason took a long breath. “We’re worried about you. Grandma calls you anorexic. And I think–”

“I do the best I can,” she cut in sharply. “And you know nothing about what I go through, so don’t judge me.”

“Can we sit down and talk before you leave?”

"Yeah, so you can repeat the words your grandma told you to tell me?"

"She has her opinion. She doesn't speak for me."

"What are you trying to tell me, Jason?"

Now's my chance.

"Maybe you shouldn't drive to work and back."

She straightened. "Have you lost your mind? I can't afford to take a taxi if that's what you're suggesting."

"The roads have black ice—"

She waggled a finger. "Uh-uh. You act like the adult admonishing me, the kid. You stick to your computer and I'll take care of my own business." She looked at Jason with a strained expression. "Grandma needs to stay out of this house if she's going to influence you, and I call what you're saying right now as siding with her on your part."

Jason's phone vibrated in his pocket.

"Answer it. If your dad pesters me one more time because you won't talk to him, I'll change my number." His mom grumbled something under her breath, put on her fur jacket, and grabbed her work bag.

"I told you. I have nothing to say to him."

"Just tell him what you want for your birthday so he'll stop texting me."

"A new car. How's that sound?"

"Don't get flippant. I'm just the messenger."

"I'm not his blood any longer. He can fricking die for all I care."

His mom paled. Her back stiffened. "Maybe those words are really meant for me instead of your dad."

"Don't twist my words around. It's dad I hate. Not you."

Jason never cried, but a lump stuck in his throat every time he remembered the day his dad left seven months before. He'd driven down the drive, waving and shouting goodbye. His mom had picked up her first bottle that day, downing the entire contents right there on the front porch. Jason had gone in the house to vomit the sadness out of his gut. He'd stayed on the bathroom floor all night long, listening to his mom cry and pace and then cry some more. After that night Jason swore he never wanted to see his dad's face again.

His mom put a finger to Jason's arm. "Are you listening to me?" She stood ramrod straight and patted wisps of hair into place as she collected herself. "Pick yourself up and move on like I did."

"You didn't move on." Jason stood his ground and decided to tell her how he really felt. "I hear you crying every time you're in your bed," he blurted. "It's all I can do to keep from punching a hole in the wall. I'll never forgive dad for doing this to you."

"I just need some more time. That's all." She swiped at a tear. "Sometimes I'm tired from the long hours I work. I'm not angry at your dad anymore though."

"Your heart's ripped open. You want things to be the same, like when dad lived here."

She bit her lower lip. "I drove him away."

"I'll never believe that. It's his fault. Not yours."

"We didn't—I didn't want—"

"Mom, stop." He put up his hand. "He fricking left and for that—he can go to hell."

She stared at the floor.

"Look. Mom. I'll make a promise to you and maybe you can make one to me."

She stared at him suspiciously. "I'm listening."

"I'll call dad if—"

Shit. I can't go there.

"If I call you when I'm leaving work?" A smile lifted the corners of her mouth. "I can do that." She took a couple of steps and embraced him. "I won't break that promise ever again."

"Okay." He took an unsteady breath. His shoulders slumped. Why didn't he have the courage to ask her to quit drinking before she killed herself? “And I won’t break mine.”

“I love you, sweetheart. Never forget that.” She sighed. “Now off to work for me.” She opened the front door, stopped, and blew a kiss. “Call your dad.”

Jason nodded and she left.

###

Jason let Sonic back in before turning on his computer. Sam wasn’t online. A Skype message popped up. He clicked on the icon.

The bastard lies in wait. Mom probably texted him.

“Turn your camera on, Jason,” his dad typed in a private message.

The almost-fifty *bastard* man who’d left with someone half his age appeared on the screen. Jason stared at his dad’s image. Bastard left just because he couldn’t keep his junk in his pants. He aimed two middle fingers at him.

“Come on, dude. I want to show you around our new place. Invite you to come and visit.”

Jason hung up and closed the window out.

“Stay out of my life, you snake,” Jason mumbled as he jumped out of the chair. He took a rolled joint out from under his mattress, opened the window, and puffed.

FEBRUARY 8

Wednesday

Sprawled out, legs atop of her favorite quilt, Samantha clicked channels.

Talk shows, news, a doctor's show about the dangers of opioids.

She pressed power. The screen blackened.

Doctor Sadana moseyed into the room and put more pamphlets on her tray. "How's our patient today?"

They all expect good, fabulous, feeling fine doc.

"Awful."

He raised a steel-wool colored eyebrow as his dark brown eyes searched hers. "That's to be expected." He put a hand to her forehead. "Headache?"

"I want to go home," she said without looking at him.

"Your heart has weakened, and fatigue has set in. You went up on the transplantation list yesterday. Once we find a match we'll need you here, not stuck in traffic." He grinned. "So, no going home right now."

Samantha didn't comment. She turned her head to glimpse the laptop screen.

No message from Jason.

He cranked his neck to see her computer. "I see you're online. Are you reading up on heart transplantation?" When she didn't answer, he nodded. "I'll leave you to rest." He left whistling.

Rest?

Tears of frustration formed. Her body ached. She lay in the sterile hospital room with an IV needle in her vein. Everyone non-medical appeared on edge, including herself.

She was alone. Her mother had gone to the cafeteria for coffee. Her concerned dad had left a phone text message saying he hoped to finish his business in Seattle by the end of the week and head home. She wanted him sitting right here beside her. What if she died during surgery?

Samantha adjusted her laptop and connected to the #heartmatch site. Jason's profile picture, showing him as connected, lifted the corners of her mouth into a smile. He'd changed the image and left a message.

She typed. *"You there?"*

As she waited her gaze took in the white room. A television hanging from a ceiling swing-arm mount, the bathroom door on the right, and the entrance door directly in front of her. An antiseptic smell permeated the room. The breakfast tray had already come and gone.

Samantha tapped the keys again. *"Sorry I missed your message. A bit busy here."* Wide-eyed emoji.

"Yep. I'm here." Jason's photo popped up. *"You wanna Skype or Facetime?"*

He can't see me like this, Samantha mouthed. *"No, thanks."* Smiley face emoji.

"You a boy in disguise?" Jason typed in.

Laughing emoji. *"Nope."*

"Married with kids?"

A shocked emoji. *"I'm eighteen, like I told you. And ugly."*

"And bald? Who cares?"

Her mother walked into the room. Samantha closed the lid.

"Are you Skyping your dad?"

"I'll catch him later." She hesitated. "Mother, could I have some privacy?"

"What?" Her mother looked momentarily taken aback then regained her composure.

"Sure. I'll go buy some magazines." She left shaking her head.

Samantha reopened the lid. She had to go back into the site. She beamed. Jason had stuck around.

"Sorry about that? My mom came in." Samantha typed.

"You at home?"

Thinker emoji. *"No."*

"You always carry your laptop with you?"

A nurse entered to draw her blood. Samantha stopped typing, closed the lid. The nurse moved her laptop to the nightstand.

Shoot. He'll get tired of these lapses in conversation and leave.

Samantha opened her computer again after the nurse left. "He's gone. Well, that's that," she uttered.

###

Jason clicked on the killer game involving lethal fun. The object of the game—stalk and chase until the kill. He could be the assassin with his dad the enemy. He'd designed a snarling photo of his dad and stuck the picture on a bobblehead-like stick figure. Jason took aim at the pathetic caricature and started shooting.

After several pleasurable hours of slaughtering his dad's image, Jason checked the bottom of his computer. Time for his mom to get off work. He lifted his gaze to stare at the window. Dark, but not snowing.

"On way," his mom texted.

"Time to clean up my act," he muttered to himself.

He picked up the clothes strewn around his room, took empty glasses and plates into the kitchen and loaded the dishwasher. Shaving and a shower came next. Just so he wouldn't look so much like his dad, he took the scissors to his hair, cutting as close to the scalp as he could.

The scraggly aftereffect made him chuckle. Next, another selfie. He changed his #heartmatch profile picture again and left a short message for Sam.

"A smile to make your day." Sounded stupid. He shrugged and decided to leave the message anyway.

Headlights lit up his bedroom wall. A car door slammed. Jason strode across his room, through the hallway, and into the living room.

He opened the front door. His mom stumbled into his arms, sobbing.

His heart picked up speed. His biggest nightmare. An accident.

"Mom, what happened?"

"I—we—"

He held her away from him, searching her face. Mascara streaked her cheeks.

"Tell me what's wrong." Jason clutched her shoulders between his hands. "Mom?"

"Your dad—"

Jason stiffened. After killing his dad over and over during the early hours of the morning, maybe he'd really died. True he hated him, but he was still his dad. Jason only wished him dead in the games. Not in real life.

"What happened to dad?" he reluctantly asked, not sure he wanted to know.

"I thought he'd come back to us. I told myself to give him a few months and he'd return."

His mom blew out a breath and hiccupped. Jason whiffed.

Damn. Whiskey this time.

She stumbled into the kitchen, crying. Jason followed and waited for her to continue.

"He always said I love you when we texted. He—, he doesn't though. I know that now."

"He doesn't?" Jason pretended ignorance.

"Matthew," she whispered. "My husband. My soulmate."

Her knees buckled. Jason grabbed her under the arms to steady her.

"Your dad—" her body leaned into Jason. "He just told me he's going to marry that girl."

His mom sank down in the closest chair. Jason's throat constricted. He'd rather have his dad dead than to see his mom hurt like this. He wrestled with the gloomy solitude of his own mind.

Bitch.

Now he'd have to kill his dad and soon to be stepmom in his games. He couldn't let this happen. He needed to figure out a way to keep his dad single. "Mom, it'll all work out. You'll see."

She opened her purse and pulled out a silver flask.

"Don't. Please," Jason begged.

She tilted the container up and guzzled. "I don't care anymore. I just don't give a shit."

Jason flinched. He'd never heard his mom cuss.

She rose and staggered out of the kitchen toward her bedroom.

His phone vibrated. He took out his cell and read.

"Answer Jason or I'll cut your phone off. I still pay most of the bills you know."

His fingers texted his dad in a fury he'd never known.

"What the shit did you just do to mom?"

"She told you, huh?"

"That piece of crap is my age. What the hell?" Jason's fingers flew over the keys.

"Don't insult Darla. She's good for me, son."

"Well, she's surely not after your dick. Maybe it's your money she wants."

A long pause before his dad answered. *"Wait until you meet her. You'll learn to love her like a mom."*

"She's twenty-five years old, for fricking sake."

"Like a sister then? Come on out, son. I want you to be my best man."

"Fricking bastard has lost it," Jason muttered.

"If you don't come to California, we'll come to you." His dad typed.

Jason pounded a fist upward wishing the air was his dad's head.

"So? What is it, Jason boy?"

"How can you hurt mom like this?"

"I fell out of love. Simple as that."

Jason didn't want to talk any more. He did want to get in the last word though.

Jason typed. *"Just go to fricking hell."*

He put his phone on Airplane Mode. If his dad called, the cell would go directly to voicemail. The urge to unfriend his dad on all his social media sites was strong, but something in his head said *not a good idea.*

Worried, he strode to his mom's bedroom to check in on her. His heart beat double-time as he eased open the door. She lay across the bed, still in her uniform. He pulled off her shoes and threw a comforter over her. He left the nightstand light on and exited the room.

###

"Damn balls are freezing," Jason said as he wrapped his comforter closer around his body and sank down on the outside back steps. He needed to smoke a joint and think.

So, dad gets his jollies from this Darla girl. He's not leaving her. Maybe if I figure out a way to make her want a younger man, she'll leave him.

Jason drew on the joint a few times. He grinned.

Ridiculous. She'd never go for me.

He laughed before continuing the conversation with himself.

And there's mom drinking herself into unconsciousness. She needs another man to make her happy. Maybe a doctor.

He toked some more. Life began to take on a new meaning. "Yep, weed makes me happy."

But first I wanna check something out.

Inside Jason checked the medicine cabinet in the main bathroom. Pulling out a bottle he read the label.

Fentanyl.

He remembered snatches of conversation between his mom and grandma when grandpa stayed here before he died of cancer. He remembered how this pill made grandpa forget his pain.

"Give him another pill." His grandma had cried.

Why does mom still have these pills? Grandpa died. She should have destroyed this container.

He gulped.

Could she be taking pills with alcohol? She's a nurse. She'd know better than to mix the two. Maybe she's planning suicide. I should hide these.

"Shit," he hissed. Jason stuck the container in the pocket of his sweats, stepped out from the bathroom, glanced in the direction of his mom's bedroom, and hurried to his room. He closed and locked the door.

After opening his computer, he went to Skype.

He private messaged his dad. *"I'm ready to talk."*

Jason waited.

His dad should be dressing for work. Tie, blue shirt, suit, perfectly shined shoes.

Yep, Mister Bastard Real Estate Agent. You can sell a house full of termites and the clients will thank you for it.

"Sup Dude?" His dad typed. *"Turn on your video."*

After turning on the video and seeing his dad's image, Jason's middle finger came up in salute.

His dad scowled. His forehead creased. "Not a nice way to say good morning," he said as he adjusted his tie. "I'm leaving for work. I can't stay in bed all day like you do."

Jason remained stony-faced. "Mom's not doing so well with this marriage thing."

"She'll get over it." He shrugged into a suit jacket then pulled his long dreadlocks back into a low hanging ponytail. He kept an eye on Jason all the while. "You get your hair cut? Looks a bit jagged. You use the scissors yourself?"

Jason stared.

When the heck did his dad get dreadlocks?

"Are you coming out for the wedding?"

Jason didn't answer because Darla pranced into the picture. Black long hair, freckles across her nose, blue eyes, and red lipstick.

Damned bitch.

"Hey, big boy," she cooed. "Your look just like your daddy."

"Jason, this is Darla. Darla—Jason."

"Come out for the wedding, Jason. You can meet my sister. She's a little older than you." Darla toyed with her hair then bent over, showing cleavage.

"I can't." Jason crossed his fingers under the desk like a six-year old would do. "I have to study."

His dad stood. "Okay. That settles it. We'll have our wedding in Denver where your mom and I married."

He's bluffing. Dad would never hurt mom like that.

"Wait, dad. Don't do anything stupid."

"Me stupid?" His dad's grin convinced Jason he'd conned him.

"Let's talk more about this later. I'll think about it."

"We planned on a Valentine's Day wedding. Got to hurry this thing up."

My birthday.

"Why that day?"

His dad laughed. "So, I'll never forget an anniversary."

Darla giggled.

"Anyway, Jase. You decide and let me know tomorrow so we can finalize our plans." His dad winked.

So, he can remember his anniversary? Nothing about my birthday?

The connection went dead.

"Dammit to hell. What the shit do I do now?"

FEBRUARY 10

Friday

Samantha's mother fidgeted nervously near the hospital window. "Your dad can't come back this weekend, sweetheart. He's heading home on Tuesday."

"No," Samantha cried out. "I want him here now. What if my surgery happens before he gets back?"

"He'll be here before surgery. No worries." She glided to the other side of the bed. "A storm's moving in. You know how your dad and I are about turbulence when flying in small airplanes." Her mother started to pet Samantha's head.

"Stop, please. My body's kinda sensitive, especially up here." Her fingers ran circles on both temples. "Daddy's not driving here?" Samantha lay back and rested her head on the pillow her mother had just fluffed.

"No. He'll turn in the rental." Her mother moved a hand to the arm bruises left by IV needles and sighed. “A friend will fly your dad back to Colorado once the weather clears.”

Samantha stared at the window then the television. “I’m so bored.” With one foot she removed the cover over her feet. She squeezed her eyes shut trying to bring her beach dream into focus. She imagined aquamarine water and pebbles peppered in the sand before her mother’s chatter broke into her fantasy.

“Should I turn on the TV?” her mother asked, placing the cover back over her feet and tucking in the ends at the foot of the bed.

Samantha sluggishly shook her head. She wanted to nap. To dream about the far-off, peaceful places she would visit one day.

Places daddy has told me about.

“Do you want to use your computer? It’s charged.”

Why should I? Jason’s not answering anymore.

After a slight knock the door opened.

“Samantha?” A woman dressed in a spotless jade green top with matching pants walked up to the bed. “My, you’re as beautiful as Doctor Sadana said you were.”

“And you are?” Samantha’s mother asked as she glanced at the nurse’s nametag.

“Ms. Wettler.” She turned to Samantha. “Please call me Elizabeth. You and I are going to be close buddies. I'll be your healthcare provider from now on."

A heartfelt smile came with the friendly face. Samantha's eyes widened. A Rock Star beautiful woman. Her eyes held a tricolored sparkle that shifted from brown to green and gold. Reddish-brown hair braided into a twist that hung at the nape of her neck. A smooth, flawless complexion and a slim figure completed her Rock Star look.

"Do I need to step out?" Samantha's mother asked.

"No need. We're off to the lab to redo a couple of Samantha's diagnostic tests and after those I want to explain the transplant procedure again." She took Samantha's hand in her own. "You'll probably have a lot of questions after we're through at the lab. I'll be at your beck and call. You can ask anything."

"I haven't seen you here before," Samantha commented.

"I've been moved from the Emergency Room to this floor. Now let me get a wheelchair and we'll head downstairs."

###

Samantha exited the lab with an oxygen mask over her face. She pointed to the mask and shrugged.

"Doctor ordered this. You've been struggling to catch a breath after the smallest exertion,"

Elizabeth explained. “End-of-stage heart failure doesn’t mean the heart is about to stop beating, but the tests showed your oxygen levels are too low.” Elizabeth pointed to the back of the chair. “You can’t see it, but there’s an oxygen tank attached back here.”

Samantha lifted the mask. “Why’d I have the shots?”

Elizabeth replaced the mask. “You don’t have to lift every time you speak. I can hear you just fine.” Elizabeth propelled the wheelchair down a pristine hall. “Vaccines decrease the chances of developing infections that can affect the transplanted heart. Any other questions, my dear?”

Samantha wavered.

Elizabeth stopped moving and faced Samantha. “Come on. Ask me.”

“For me to survive someone has to die. That makes me sad.” Tears welled. Her throat constricted as she held back the urge to cry.

Elizabeth crouched in front of her and clasped Samantha’s hands. “There are many of us on an organ donor list. If I died tomorrow, just knowing someone could live because I’m willing to give an organ, well—that knowledge gives me peace.”

Samantha gripped Elizabeth’s hands tightly and sighed.

"You have to be a little egoistic. And besides, don't you want an improvement in the quality of your life?" The nurse patted her hand then gently released her and stood before changing the subject. "Do you have a boyfriend?"

"No," Samantha said quietly.

"And why is that?" Elizabeth prompted. "I would bet it's because you never go out." She moved to the back of the wheelchair and began pushing.

"My mother home schools me."

"Surely you use the computer to communicate with friends."

"My friends stopped coming over. And yes, sometimes I meet people online."

"Well, there you have it. Get better and eventually seek those friends out."

"Could I ask a favor?"

"If it's not for barbequed ribs, go ahead."

"Could you call me Sammy?"

"Can do." Elizabeth squeezed Samantha's shoulder.

###

Weak winter sunlight melted some snow off the sidewalks. Jason's mom had recently started a day shift, easing his mind to some extent. He'd been consumed with boredom at the house, so he'd grabbed his skateboard and spent the morning at the skate park. Sonic ran with him.

His phone vibrated in his left pocket.

Ignore. It's dad.

The other pocket held his securities. A rolled joint and one Fentanyl tablet.

He'd been a boarder for years. What he liked most about boarding was he could do the sport he loved alone and never talk to another person. That's the way he wanted it.

You don't bother me and I'll leave you alone too.

This passion of his had kept him sane after his dad left.

Around noontime Jason skated home, fixed a sandwich, opened a soda, and headed straight to his room. He moved the mouse to light the laptop's screen.

Shit.

Another message from his dad. He clicked.

"It's Darla. You there?"

"What the fricking bullshit is dad gonna try now?" He turned the video on.

"Pass me to my dad," Jason ordered.

"He's at work. Can you and I chat for a while?"

"She's hitting on me," he said under his breath. At least her boobs weren't hanging out this time.

"We've got nothing to say to each other," Jason uttered.

"Look Jason. You don't know me, so don't judge." She took in a breath. "My dad died when I turned nine. Heart attack. There one day, gone the next."

"So that's why you go for older men?" He scowled hoping she'd see his disgust.

"Maybe. Although I didn't break up your mom and dad's marriage."

"I think you did. He's got money, you've got looks. You pulled him in like a sucker on a fish line."

"What I do have is a university education and that's what I wanted to talk to you about," Darla said.

"Not interested."

"One day you'll wish you hadn't frittered your time away."

"Look. No preaching. I'm done. Outta here." Jason started to disconnect.

"Don't go. I'll change the subject. Just give me ten more minutes."

He glared at the screen.

"Please be our best man at the wedding. I'm not interested where the ceremony takes place.

Here or there for all I care. Wherever would make your dad happy. He loves you so much."

"Like crap he does."

"Jase—"

"Don't call me that. I'm Jason to you."

"Sorry. I didn't mean to hurt your feelings."

"You fricking hurt my feelings when you stole dad and my mom changed."

"Rethink what you just said, Jason."

She got closer to the screen. He automatically scooted back.

"I did not kidnap your dad. That's just a ridiculous statement. He's almost fifty, for gosh sake. He can make up his own mind."

Jason wanted a smoke. He took the joint out and looked in the drawer for a lighter.

"Your mom changed? I'm sorry. That's not my fault either."

Where's my lighter?

She tapped the screen. "Listen to me."

He looked up.

"Just love and support her. Be the man in this picture. She might not be around forever, you know."

Jason flicked the lighter and drew on the stub.

"And that, right there," she pointed to the joint, "repulses me. Grow up."

She broke the connection. The screen darkened.

Shit. Now she'll tell dad.

###

Samantha switched off the television when she grew tired of hearing about the worst storm in decades getting closer to Denver.

"Mother," she whispered to the woman dozing in a chair beside her bed. "Hey."

She jumped. "What's wrong, my dear? Need to go to the bathroom?"

"Go get something to eat. You've been up here all day."

"No, sweetheart. I'm fine. Really."

"I just need some time to myself," Samantha lied.

"Oh." She checked her phone. "Okay. Text me if you need anything. Promise?"

"Promise, mother."

She placed the laptop on Samantha's thighs before she left.

Can't fool her anymore.

Samantha opened her computer and clicked on the #heartmatch site.

"Are you back yet?" she typed. *"Can you talk?"* Jason hadn't been online for days.

"I'm here. Don't wanna talk though."

Jason's happy face profile picture didn't fit the tone of the words he typed in.

"Something not right?" Emoji sending a hug appeared.

"Just about everything. Today I'm on this earth. Tomorrow, who knows?" He wrote.

"You're alive. That counts." Samantha had a hard time listening to the complaints of others. To her—she just wanted to live. She typed. *"Jason do you believe in fate?"*

"It's called coincidence." A lengthy pause before he went on. *"If I get hit by a flying flowerpot as I walk down the block—it happened by chance."*

"That's fate." Samantha typed. *"Hey, let's Facetime."* After she hit send, Samantha winced, unsure about seeing him face-to-face. If he accepted her offer of Facetiming, he'd soon find out everything about her.

A smiling face emoji popped up. Samantha giggled. *"You just sent me an emoji?"* She wrote and grinned.

"Let's exchange numbers," he typed.

One minute later, Samantha's phone rang. She answered the Facetime call.

"Hey, nothing's ugly so far," Jason said.

She moved her phone around the room. “This is where I live.”

“In a bedroom?” he asked.

“A hospital room.”

His brows furrowed.

“What happened? You have an accident?”

“I’m dying, Jason.”

She moved the phone to her IV, the heart monitor machine, her face.

Her voice trembled with emotion. “If I want to live, someone dies.”

“I don’t get it.” His stare sharpened. His gray eyes darkened. “Sam, I mean ah—” he paused. “I’m not feeling too well. I gotta go.”

Jason disconnected.

###

The screen image had mesmerized Jason. He couldn’t tear his thoughts away from the impression she’d left. On his run to the bathroom, he tripped. His guts erupted and vomit, spewing like lava, landed everywhere.

He pulled the Fentanyl tablet from his pocket, crawled to the bathroom, stood before the mirror, cupped his hands to drink, and washed the medicine down his throat.

“Sleep. That’s all I want right now,” he moaned before throwing up again. “What the fricking crap just happened?”

He laid on his back, head in his own puke, legs spread, glaring at the ceiling. The word fate crossed his mind before he gave the air his middle finger.

###

After cleaning up the mess, Jason showered and stood outside with Sonic while his dog looked for a place to poop. With only his boxers on, the freezing air numbed Jason's extremities. He huffed trying to warm his fingers.

Sonic scooted back inside. For a split-second Jason imagined the door shutting, locking him outside. He shivered at the thought. He'd been locked out before, right after his dad had disappeared from his life.

He slipped into a pair of jeans and a Polo sweater and sat behind his computer screen.

According to California time his dad should be home. Jason had to give him an answer about the wedding. His mom texted she'd be working extra hours, so he wouldn't have to worry about her for the moment. He clicked on Skype and his dad's connection.

It rang several times.

The picture came into view and there sat Darla, all goody-goody, with her arms folded in front of her.

"Your dad's working overtime. I'll tell him you called."

"Ah–, I–"

"You Skyped to tell him about the wedding, right?"

"Un-huh."

"I can imagine your answer," she smirked.

That's it.

"You don't know shit about me and don't fricking listen to what my dad says."

"Your dad? You're all he ever talks about. He says, 'I miss him so damn much. I can't sleep. I can't eat.'" She mimicked in a low voice. "I hear that day in and out."

"Then he shoulda stayed here."

Darla shook her head. "You don't get it. He fell out of love with your mom. There's no going back. Ever. Got that?"

"Dad screwed you before he left mom. If you hadn't–"

"He didn't. I wouldn't let him near me until he showed me the divorce papers. Believe me or not." She homed in on his stare. "My mom taught me better than that."

Jason dropped his gaze and fiddled with the bottom of his shirt. When he lifted his chin again, Darla smiled.

"Get to know me, Jason. You might end up liking me." She paused for a moment. "I'll tell you what. I'll talk your dad into marrying me here. Justice of the Peace. We've done the paperwork. Easy peasy."

He became suspicious. "And then?"

"He leaves right after the wedding and spends your birthday with you. Alone, just the two of you."

Jason shrugged his shoulders. "Why would you do that?"

"You both need some time together. To talk things through so that the past can close and the future can open." She inhaled deeply and let her breath out slowly. "Better for everyone. Maybe even your mom."

Shit now I really need a joint.

"Did grandma Rosie call you?"

"She's called. She won't talk to me."

"Do you think dad will go for coming here?"

"He will. Trust me."

"You're pretty sure of yourself." A slight smile lifted the corners of Jason's mouth.

"I'll do this one thing for you because you're a good kid who just wants what's best for his mom." She thought for a bit. "Kinda like me."

Jason lifted his arms in question.

"My sister and I are all my mom has. She never married again after dad died. She lives a sad, lonely life now that my sister and I have left home and she's all alone. Don't let your mom turn out the same way."

"My mom's become an alcoholic," Jason confessed.

Darla nodded. "Sadness and loneliness can do that to a person."

"She won't get help."

"Probably because she truly believes she can stop any time she wants."

He nodded.

"Hey, your dad's coming in. Want to talk to him?"

"Not today. Maybe tomorrow."

"He won't bite you know."

"Yep, I get that. I'm still mad at him, that's all."

She grinned and covered her mouth with her hand, whispering. "Okay, let's talk tomorrow and I'll tell you when he'll arrive in Colorado."

"Okay."

The image disconnected.

FEBRUARY 11

Saturday

Samantha finished her lunch, put her computer on the tray beside her plate, and pushed the cart away. Earlier Nurse Elizabeth had given her a sponge bath. Her mother had gone to the hospital's chapel. The television showed only news and upcoming hockey games.

Her laptop chimed. She turned toward the screen.

Skype. It's daddy.

She put a hand to her chest to still the flutters. Maybe her stomach gave those signals and not her heart.

She pulled the cart over to her bed and clicked. His video picture popped up.

My handsome daddy.

Of Swedish decent. Laugh lines decorated the corners of the most gorgeous green eyes. A smile that exhibited perfect teeth. The towering height of a professional basketball player.

"Hey there baby girl." A smile lightened his concerned gaze. "That mask is becoming. You're even more beautiful."

"I'm number one on the wait list." Samantha sighed. "Doctor Sadana said I had to stay in the hospital." Her throat tightened. Tears welled. "Hurry home daddy. Please. You'll be here with me during the operation, won't you?"

"Yes, my love. I'm leaving Tuesday morning. Weather permitting, I'll land in time to share lunch with you."

"Tuesday," she gasped. "What if my donor—"

I can't say that word.

"Sweetheart?"

"Yes, daddy."

"I hope guilt isn't taking over your thoughts."

Samantha disregarded his question. "There's a storm coming. Did you forget Tuesday is the fourteenth? Valentine's Day?"

"That blasted storm's why we're waiting. Rest assured. The snow tempest is predicted for tomorrow. Monday should be a good, clear day and just to make sure, we're leaving Tuesday, which will be an even better day to fly." He grinned. "I wouldn't miss one more special day with the other love of my life."

Samantha glanced outside. “There are no clouds in the sky. Please come home today.”

“I can’t. I’ve got some important documents to finish up before I return.”

“Papers are more important than me?”

“Honey, some of my people could be deported if I take off today and leave them hanging.”

“It’s Saturday. When you’re here you don’t work on the weekend.”

“Sammy.” He reached out a finger out as if to caress her cheek. “I’ll be there. Trust me. You just take care of yourself and your mother. Besides, you can watch us fly.”

“Facetiming while you’re in the air?” She smiled. Her daddy always made her smile.

“Yep. That’s right.”

Her nurse tiptoed into the room.

“Is that Nurse Elizabeth I see in the background?”

Samantha nodded.

“Miss Elizabeth, take care of my baby girl until I get back,” her dad teased. “Okay, Sweet Pea. I have some paperwork to catch up on and—”

“Can’t you stay online for a while longer?”

“I wish I could. I’ll Skype you tomorrow and Monday and Facetime Tuesday as we’re departing." He kissed his fingertips and touched the screen.

"Bye." Samantha closed the lid and sighed wistfully.

I've always been my daddy's girl.

She fretted whenever her dad was out of town. He tucked her in every single night, except for when he worked away from home.

Elizabeth checked the IV drip, then took her blood pressure and temperature. The nurse's head bobbed absentmindedly.

Is she talking to herself? Did I just hear her say the word bitch?

"Everything's looking good." Her nurse smiled. "Do your friends call you Sammy?"

Samantha shook her head. "That nickname's reserved for special people."

"Well then, I'll thank you for the exceptional compliment, my dear."

Elizabeth went around Samantha's bed tucking in the sheets and smoothing the quilt."

"I love the photos of you. This one is so cute." She motioned to a picture of Samantha and her parents, taken during a thirteenth birthday party.

"If you don't mind my asking, what's your dad do?"

"He's a lawyer."

"Does he travel a lot?"

"Un-huh. He works with immigrants and their rights."

Elizabeth nodded. "And your mother?"

"She used to teach at a university. Now she home schools me."

"Could I put your laptop away?"

"Not yet. There's someone I want to chat with after—"

"After I leave the room?" Elizabeth smiled then checked her watch. "I'll be back in thirty minutes."

"If you see my mother along the way, could you keep her out? I mean like distract her?"

"Yes, Sammy." Elizabeth laughed. "I'll keep her occupied with some of my own stories."

"Elizabeth?" Samantha rested a hand on her breast.

"Yes, dear."

"My chest hurts."

"Are you sure it's a physical pain?"

"I think so." Samantha swiped at her face as tears trickled down her cheeks.

Elizabeth nodded and put her stethoscope eartips in her ears then placed the cold metal against her chest. After listening, she laid her hand on Samantha's arm. "I think you're missing your dad. To be safe, try not to talk too much and keep that mask on. I'll be at the nurse's desk. When I come back I'll recheck your vitals."

Elizabeth put the call button in her hand.

"Press this if your pain gets worse. I'll be right outside."

###

Jason showered. He took the Fentanyl pill bottle out of hiding and tossed the container into his desk. He left his room and went through the kitchen to open the back door for Sonic. Gray clouds hung over the mountains.

A gust of freezing air hit his bare chest. He clutched the lapels of his robe closed as he waited for his dog to circle around and do his business. Grandma Rosie came through the back gate. Jason waved and opened the door wider. Sonic couldn't get through the opening fast enough and grandma scooted inside right behind the dog.

Grandma Rosie's cold hands squeezed Jason's cheeks together, making his lips pucker up, ready for the wet kiss she always gave him. Her close-cropped frizzy hair had turned gray after Grandpa died. Although outwardly her zest for life had never waned, Jason knew she hid an inner sadness. Was it because of grandpa, or because his dad had abandoned them? She scanned the kitchen.

"You're such a big help to your mom." Her chestnut-colored eyes glistened. "Your dad never lifted a finger to help me."

"That's because you spoiled him, grandma."

She playfully smacked his behind.

"You're naked under there. Get some clothes on while I fix you something to eat."

"I've got boxers on." Jason contemplated his next words. "Grandma? Could I talk to you about mom?"

"Sure Jason. We can chat while I busy myself around the stove. Aren't you freezing? Run to your bedroom and put on that flannel shirt I got you and something to cover your legs. That'll warm you up."

"Back in five."

Jason heard the Skype ring as he strode down the hallway. He raced into his room and closed the door.

Sam. Yep. It's Sam alright.

He lowered the volume and adjusted the video.

"Hey, you barely caught me," he said.

She had a frail look about her. The mask rested below her chin.

"Just checking in." She put a hand to her chest.

"You okay today?"

"I have bad days." She slid on the mask. "And I have worse days."

"You're waiting for a transplant, aren't you?"

A slight nod of her head.

"Does talking hurt you?"

Her gaze lifted. Sam's eyes were the color of turquoise. Her complexion, chalk white. He watched her take some breaths. His mom had taught him how to take a pulse. He counted the heaves of her chest as he kept an eye on the second hand of his watch. "No fever."

"Huh?"

"Nothing. Just talkin to myself. Hey Sam. If–"

She waggled a finger at him and put her palm into the stop position.

"You don't like the nickname Sam?"

"No," she mouthed.

"What about Princess Sam?"

Finger wagged, although she smiled under the mask.

"Anyway, I can talk for you today." He inhaled deeply and let his breath out slowly. Shake your head if you don't want to hear me out. Okay?"

She nodded.

"Let's see. How about I tell you something about me?"

She dipped her head a bit.

Maybe that's a yes.

"Well, I'm single. Never cared much for girls," he lifted his gaze, "until now."

Shit. Why'd I say that?

Samantha grinned. He loved her smile.

"I love skate-boarding, my killer games on the computer, and smoking weed." He stared waiting for her reaction.

She shrugged.

"I have a dog named Sonic." He turned indicating the bed and moved his computer around, so Samantha could see Sonic. "I rescued him about five years ago."

He looked at the ceiling trying to think of more information to give her.

"Your parents?"

"I come from a bi-racial family." He put a finger on his chin.

"Siblings?" Samantha asked.

"I had a younger brother. He died a long time ago. Choked to death. That's why my mom's so protective."

"Your dad?"

"My dad left my mom and me last year after I graduated."

"Oh," her mouth formed a perfect circle.

"It fricking sucks not having him around." His gaze caught and held Samantha's. "Boring?"

"No." Samantha rested her head on her pillow.

"My dad wants me to go to his wedding in California. If I go, my mom would lose it." He lowered his glance, embarrassed with the details he had never told anyone before.

She swiped at a tear.

"Hey, is that for me?"

She nodded. "I don't know what I'd do if my dad weren't around." She laid a hand on her chest again. "I feel the pain here," her hand moved to her heart area, "when he's gone. And I shouldn't be stressed." She sniffed. "It's not good for the remainder of my heart." She went on. "Tell me about your mom."

"My mom's not doing so well with that fricking wedding happening in three days. My parents are divorced and her broken—" he caught himself before he said the word heart. "She thinks he'll come back."

His grandma knocked on the door.

"Can we talk later, Sam?"

She frowned.

"Oops. I'm sorry. I forgot. I'll think of something else to call you."

Jason disconnected and closed the lid.

"Coming," he hollered.

###

A waldorf salad, a baked potato swathed in butter, green beans, and his favorite—a grilled steak, awaited him at the kitchen table.

"Aren't you eating, grandma?" Jason sat behind the meal.

"That's mine. Yours is a bowl of oatmeal." She hurried to the stovetop and got a steaming china dish. She couldn't hold in her chuckles as she plopped down beside him.

He cut into the medium rare piece of meat as she spooned the cereal.

His grandma watched him closely. "The news says it's going to snow real bad. Did you see those clouds out there?" She pointed.

Jason nodded.

His grandma laughed. "Oh, I know how that old saying goes. 'Talk at the table, sing in bed and the goblins will git ya while you sleep.'"

Jason grinned. "That's not how that rhyme goes." He smiled before he stuck another piece of steak into his mouth.

After the meal, his grandma got up and started clearing the plates.

Jason touched her arm. "I'll get those later. Sit down and listen to me." After one of her brows arched he uttered, "please."

She sat.

"Mom's guzzling alcohol and she's doing most of her drinking on her drive home from work."

"I've known about your mom's drinking for quite a while, Jason."

"Why didn't you say anything?"

"For the same reason you haven't. Her heart's shattered. How can I tell her to put away her security blanket?"

"But she's drinking and driving, grandma. She'll kill herself someday."

"Or someone else," his grandma agreed. "It's your dad's fault." Grandma slammed the flat of her hand on the table. Her forehead wrinkled and her pupils contracted into pinpoint holes in her anger. "Blast it to high heaven."

"Don't get mad at me."

"No, sweetheart." She rested a hand on Jason's arm. "I'm not angry at you. I don't claim your dad anymore. He did a God-awful thing when he left your mom after twenty-some years. You," she squinted. "Well, you can manage on your own, though I'm sure your mom will never be able to start over like he's doing."

"I sure don't want to see him any time soon."

Unless he comes alone like Darla promised.

Grandma stared at him briefly before continuing. "I've cursed, fretted, and cried about your dad leaving. Matthew told me on the phone he's moving on. Nothing more I can do about him."

Jason inhaled deeply. His jaw clenched before he released the air. "What can I do?"

"Should we make an anonymous call to her supervisor at the hospital?"

He shook his head. "That's not the answer."

"I could talk to her."

"Grandma, that won't work. She's closed herself off, especially after dad told her he's getting married."

"Her name's Darla, right?"

"Yep."

"What if your dad comes back here alone and talks to her?"

"That's something I'm—"

Grandma interrupted. "I could call this Darla woman and tell her to stay away from him."

Jason moved his chair away from the table and stood. "I spoke to her. Alone. She didn't seem too bad."

"You're talking to your dad's mistress?"

"Mom and dad have some issues to settle. I'm just trying to get dad back here by himself. Darla promised to ask him for me."

"You don't want to call your dad and ask him yourself?"

Jason grit his teeth. "Not yet. I'm still pissed about everything's he's done to mom."

"And you've suffered too. You hardly ever go out anymore."

"What if dad returns and mom thinks he's come back to make up to her?"

"My hope is that he'll do just that. He'll soon tire of that youngin," his grandma concluded. She squeezed his hand. "You're such an intelligent young lad. I know you'll figure everything out to save your mom." Grandma got teary-eyed. "I'm glad you don't do drugs, watch—"

"Grandma. Don't go there. Not today anyway." He strode across the kitchen. "Back to my computer."

"I'll tidy up in here. Your mom's due home shortly and I want to be out of here before she gets back."

"Scared?" He grinned.

"No. I'd get mad and tell her I know she's tipping the bottle." Her gaze engulfed his. "Can't you level with her?"

Jason shook his head and grew solemn. "I sure miss grandpa. He would've kept dad walking a straight line."

"Don't worry. Grandpa's got his eye on things."

Back in his room, Jason opened the desk drawer and took out the prescription bottle. He rolled the container around in the palms of both hands. The pills clicked against the plastic.

"What if something happened to me? Would dad rush back?"

So, if Darla's plan didn't work, he had this option to ponder.

He glanced upwards.

Does grandma really believe that grandpa's watching over us?

Jason opened his game.

I want blood.

This time, Jason turned up the action. He cut his dad out of the perimeter and invented other characters. They ran around corners, over bridges, down dark alleyways trying to get away from him, the shooter. Jason stalked them for hours and shot carefully, wounding them.

After a while, he tracked down and maimed characters and this time, aimed for the kill. The blood he thirsted for became a fulfillment. Like a shot of adrenaline that made him high.

His anger only marginally satisfied, he finished up his game and then started another, ramping up the action even more. He'd get what that bastard had done out of his head one way or another.

###

Hours later the front door slammed. "Mom," he mouthed and jumped to his feet. He'd lost track of time.

He put the pill bottle deep into his pocket and strode out of his room. They bumped into each other at the end of the hallway. She screeched, and he cursed.

"You scared me," his mom said as she slipped a crinkled bag into her daypack.

Jason knew what brown paper bags held. "And you stepped on my foot."

"It's winter. Wear slippers."

"You're supposed to text when you leave work."

"I need a shower. Some heavy stuff going on at work."

She took two steps before he gripped her arm. His mom glanced at his hand before she looked straight into his eyes.

"Just want to make your load lighter." Jason straightened his stance, let go of his mom's arm, and grasped the shoulder strap.

"What are you doing? I need to study some documents."

"While you're under the shower's hot spray?" Jason taunted.

Her eyes closed to slits. "Has grandma been talking to you?"

"No. Actually mom, I've been talkin' to her."

His mom began to shake. "You're chatting with grandma behind my back?" Her lip quivered as tears welled. "I'm just trying to make it, Jase and I can't without this." She pointed to the bag as tears coursed down her face. "So now you know. It's a little something that helps me forget."

"I've known for some time, mom."

"Okay. So, give me the bag and I'll go do what I do best."

"You can keep whatever's in here but do your drinking here at home. Not on the road."

The tears stopped. "Well," she huffed. "Those words didn't come from your mouth. Who told you to say that to me?"

"No one tells me what to say. I just know what I've seen. I worry about your drivin' and drinkin'. What if you have an accident and die?"

His mom stared at him.

"That could happen, you know."

Her gaze was emotionless. "I can stop any time I want. After all, it's not like I'm an alcoholic."

"You don't eat right and you drink yourself to sleep. You need to get some help."

"No one notices. I just sip when I'm on break and—"

"Jeez." Jason threw his arms up in the air. "While you're working? Is that why you were transferred out of the ER? Someone's keeping an eye on you," he stated emphatically.

A feeble smile crossed her lips. "I've never bungled anything at work. I'm praised for the way I take care of my patients. The transfer came along with a raise. And now," she took in a trembling breath, "now I can finally pay the mortgage without running short every month."

"We don't have to live here, mom. We can move to an apartment. I'll find a job to help out with the expenses."

Her heart-wrenching stare fixated on something behind him. Jason turned.

He gasped. "Why'd you put that up?"

She shrugged and began to cry. "It feels like I've lost everyone I've ever loved."

"You have me. And Grandma Rosie. We'll never leave you."

Her eyes became expressionless. "Darin had just turned five. I knew he shouldn't play and eat a hard candy at the same time. I turned my back to pick up toys and when I couldn't find him—"

She'd retreated to the past. Jason knew this story and the real reason his mom had become a nurse.

"Mom, accidents happen," Jason stated.

"He hid under the bed, on his back, and the candy lodged in his throat. I didn't know what to do when I found him." She buried her face in her hands and cried. "He had turned blue."

"Mom, please."

"Everything's my fault," she whispered.

To Jason, she seemed shattered. More so than he'd ever seen her before. He tried to embrace her and when that didn't work, he grasped her hand. She shook free and fled to the solitude of her room, choosing a bottle of alcohol over his comfort.

He returned to the photo on the wall, stroked his brother's face with the tips of his fingers, and smiled. Darin sat on dad's lap and mom, standing behind with Jason, had one arm around him and the other holding little Darin's hand.

Happier times.

FEBRUARY 12

Sunday

A shiver rippled over Samantha's skin. A feeling of panic and helplessness overwhelmed her after awakening from a nightmare that still lay at the edge of her memory. Crowds of people milling around in a vapor. Her dad calling out her name and extending his hand for help. Her inability to reach him from the constraints of her wheelchair.

She glanced around her room as near total darkness surrounded her. The early morning din in the hallway as nurses prepared to leave their night shifts eased her mind. Glass containers clinked on moveable trays rolling down the hallway. The low hum of a vacuum came from somewhere in the distance and the smell of pancakes wafted through the air.

I'm not alone.

She reached for her phone. She'd left the cell charging against Nurse Elizabeth's advice. *"No electronic devices near your bed."* And Elizabeth gave that same constant reminder every evening, before tuck-in time. The evening before, after a call to her dad, she'd hidden her cell under the pillow.

She pushed contacts and then favorites to bring up her dad's name. She pressed Facetime.

Daddy, please answer. I need to see you.

"Hey there precious."

Shoot, he's still in bed. I forgot Seattle time. An hour behind.

"Everything okay?" He yawned and scrubbed his head.

"I had a bad dream, daddy."

"About me?" He pinched his cheek then grinned at her. "See Sammy, I'm fine."

"Want me to call you back after you get up?"

"Absolutely not." She watched as he pulled the covers up to his chin and snuggled in, holding the phone in front of him. "Tell me about your dream."

"I couldn't get out of my wheelchair and—"

"Sweetheart, look me in the eye." His phone narrowed in to expose one sea-green eye then her dad winked. "I'll be with you Tuesday. Relax. Nothing's going to happen to me." He moved his cell back to arm's length.

Don't cry.

Samantha inhaled and released her breath slowly. “I’m scared, daddy.”

“I know you are my precious. I would be too if I were in that same hospital.”

Samantha lifted her mask off. A sob caught in her throat.

“No, I mean—you’re in the best hospital in the world. It’s the wait that makes you more frightened, right?”

Samantha didn’t respond. She looked down and fingered the photos on her quilt.

“Your mom and I will be right next to you throughout everything, even recovery.” He smiled. “And guess what?”

Her gaze lifted. “What?”

“I’m taking two months off after you have your surgery.” His deep smile lifted her spirits. “You will beg me to get out of your sight after spending that much time with me.”

She grinned and put her mask back in place.

“That’s my girl.” He scratched his cheek. “What time will mom come back this morning?”

“After breakfast and my bath.”

“Does Nurse Elizabeth stay the night?”

“No, she doesn’t. She’s already here this morning though. She peeked in and blew a kiss before I called you.”

Samantha wanted to keep his face in front of her all day. She relaxed as her fear began to dissolve.

"Is snow on the ground yet?"

She glanced outside. Flakes blew sideways. She could hardly see the street light. "I can't see the ground but yes, it's snowing."

"You see? The blizzard is supposed to move out some time during the night. We'll be ready to go when the time's right. I'll bring you a special present," he added as an afterthought.

She smiled again, for his benefit. Then her lips wavered. Samantha didn't know how to keep that fake grin plastered on when thinking about her daddy's safety.

"Promise you'll Facetime me while flying?"

"You're already worrying about the day after tomorrow? Honey, Dale has been airborne with Cessnas for forty years. He's an expert. And sweetheart, I'll do my best to Facetime you along the way if reception's possible. Okay?"

She nodded.

"Believe in me?"

Her head bobbed, though she didn't feel enthusiastic.

"Now," he brought his phone back in to plant a kiss and moved the cell away again. "I can get a couple more hours sleep. We can Skype later. How's that?"

"Okay."

"Love you, my precious. You and your mom are my life. Don't forget that."

"I won't, daddy. I love you too."

She disconnected.

Samantha pressed contacts. Pulled up Jason's number and called.

He picked up on the second ring.

"Sup, Princess?"

"What?"

He grinned. "You know. What's crackalackin?"

"Jason, are you high?"

A hearty, deep chuckle erupted. "What's happening. It's teen slang, Princess."

She lifted her shoulders in a shrug. "Did I wake you?"

"No, I got off my computer to fix mom some breakfast before she went to work."

"You haven't been to bed?"

"Nope."

"Games?"

"Yep." He smiled. "Enough about me. How are you today, Princess?"

"Feeling kinda down this morning."

"You hurtin somewhere?"

"In my head. At least that's where my pain seems to be right now."

"Headache?"

"No. I'm worried about my dad. He's coming in from Seattle."

"Driving? Flying?"

"Flying with a friend. It's snowing here and I'm so worried something will happen."

"A small plane?"

"Yes. That's why I'm afraid."

"Well, I'm sure his friend won't fly if the weather's bad and hey—if you want to feel better, Tuesday's my birthday."

"Really? You'll be twenty on Valentine's Day?"

"Yep. Want to celebrate with me?"

"What do you mean?"

"I could bring you a slice of cake."

She snickered. "You'd do that for me?"

"Yep. Just tell me the name of your hospital and I'll bring a big piece of chocolate, slathered in white frosting."

While Samantha could Facetime or Skype Jason, she didn't want him to see her in person, yet. That could come later, after she'd washed her hair, wore real clothes, and had a new heart.

She hesitated before answering. Right now, she had no friends except for Jason. She didn't want to lose him.

"Maybe your parents wouldn't like me because I'm mixed?"

"Oh no," she blurted out. "My dad works with immigrants. My parents are pretty liberal and celebrate diversity. It's just—"

"You don't want me to see you like this?"

Samantha nodded shyly.

"Well, I get that." He seemed pensive. "Listen. About this fate thing. You know I don't believe in it, right?"

"Un-huh."

"So, don't try to convince me."

"Why would I do that?"

"Don't know. Maybe one day you might try to say we met for a reason."

One day? He said one day? He's planning on keeping me around?

"Each to his own belief. That's what my mom always taught me. Oh, and daddy says to never judge anyone. No one is perfect."

Jason pondered. "Do your parents have names?"

She laughed. "My mother is Jenny. My dad is Benjamin. Ben for short."

"I'd like to meet your parents someday. I'll bet they're sick."

"What? There's nothing wrong with either of them. Why'd you say that?"

Jason's eyes widened. "Do friends visit you?"

"Not anymore."

"Okay, I get it." He leaned in. Put his face up close so she could only see his mouth move. "Sick means cool, awesome."

Samantha giggled. Her mask steamed from her expulsion of breath.

"You have a nice smile."

"Thanks. I've changed my mind. You can call me Sam after all."

"Okay, and Jason is still my name."

"You don't have a nickname?"

"My dad calls me Jase." He thought for a moment. "And sometimes my mom does too. I don't like it though. My grandpa was Jason."

She nodded. Jason's expression had drooped when he spoke about his grandpa.

Maybe he'd died.

"Keep smiling, Sam."

"Can we talk later? My nurse will be in any minute."

"Sure. This afternoon?"

"Sounds good." She turned her phone off.

Nurse Elizabeth walked into her room seconds later.

"Your dad?"

Samantha nodded.

"Okay. Let's take your vitals and get you bathed before your mom comes to visit. How about I wash your hair today?"

"Okay." She'd need a nap after that.

So tired and I just woke.

###

Jason's phone pinged. He looked at a text from Darla asking him to call her while his dad was out playing racquetball at the gym. She included her cell number under the text.

He put her number into his contacts and pressed the Facetime call button. She picked up on the first ring.

"That's the fastest I've ever had a call back." She smiled.

"Sup?" Jason's curiosity got the best of him.

"Your dad and I got married late yesterday evening."

"And he's at the gym? That's weird."

"Facts of life," Darla said. "We've been living together for months. He has to have his weekend workout, so off he went."

"Did you do the white dress thing?"

“No. We’ll catch up on that stuff later. Judges don’t care. They just want the ceremony over with. More clients, more money for them.”

“What’s next?”

“Your dad’s heading out tomorrow after he shows a house. Probably late morning. It’ll take a little over fourteen hours to get to Colorado.”

“With stops that means more like sixteen hours.”

“That’s right.”

“Does he know it’s snowing here?”

“He knows. He’ll stop if the weather gets too bad. Told me he’s a good driver and not to mention the driving part again.”

“He’s okay coming alone?”

“Your dad got mad at me for scheming behind his back. After an evening of arguing, he agreed seeing you might be the best thing to do.”

“You argued before you got married?”

“No, the other way around,” she laughed.

“You okay with everything?”

She shrugged. “We’ve been together every day since we came to California. Right now, I don’t know how I feel about this trip. I’m making a sacrifice for you, Jason.”

“I’ll owe you.”

"Payback will be a visit to Los Angeles next summer, meeting my sister, and thinking about going to the university out here."

"Did dad tell you he wanted me to move?"

"I kinda suggested that if your relationship improved, you might like to study in the sun."

He grimaced.

Shit.

"I should probably call back later and talk to dad."

"Up to you."

"Okay. I'll think about it. Over and out?"

She disconnected. Darla didn't seem too convinced about his dad's trip.

And I'll never leave the mountains for the ocean.

###

Samantha opened her eyes from a nap and met Elizabeth's gaze.

"You kept moaning in your sleep, Sammy. Bad dream?"

Samantha picked a point on the wall, someplace over Elizabeth's shoulder and stared at it.

"Come on. We can talk through whatever's bothering you."

Samantha shrugged. "Daddy's flying in on Tuesday."

"So why the solemn expression?"

"I'm not feeling good about the flight. He says the storm will be over by then. What if he crashes?"

Elizabeth rested her hand on Samantha's arm. "You can't *what if* every time a situation arises, my dear. You'll never rest easy under those circumstances."

Samantha cast a skeptical eye at her.

"Everything about life should be taken day-by-day. You wake up in the morning and you smile because it's a new day. When you go to sleep at night, you're grateful for the good things that have happened during the day."

Samantha watched as Elizabeth's face suddenly hardened. A vertical frown line appeared between her brows as if something had clicked in her mind about what she'd just said.

"What if it's not all good?"

She patted Samantha's arm. "You're right. Sometimes things happen for a reason and there's no justification as to why they happen the way they do."

"So, what if I die during surgery? Isn't that fate?" She glanced upwards. "Doesn't somebody up there already know what's going to happen to me?"

"That's where trust comes into the equation. Your doctors are the best in the world. They will use all of their skills to make your new heart function for you."

"Has everything always worked out for you?"

Elizabeth shook her head. She broke eye contact and looked away then focused on an empty space between her hands and deliberated a moment before she answered. "No, it hasn't and I didn't handle my situation well at all."

"How did you learn to manage your problem?"

"I didn't. I'm still in mourning."

"Someone died?"

"No, someone left me."

"Can't you take your own advice? Go day-by-day and be grateful for what you have?"

Elizabeth's head jerked up. Tears welled and then ran down her cheeks. She swiped them away.

Samantha reached out and touched Elizabeth's arm. "I'm sorry. I didn't mean to make you cry."

"I'll be fine. Just give me five minutes to freshen up in the bathroom and I'll be back to normal."

With that Elizabeth jumped up, grabbed her daypack from the floor, and ran out of the room.

###

Thirty minutes later, Elizabeth reentered Samantha's room. She smiled.

"I am grateful for what I have. A loving son, a mother-in-law who sometimes loves and supports me, and now I have you. What more could I ask for?"

Doctor Sadana moseyed into the room and laid a hand on Elizabeth's shoulder.

"How's our patient today?"

Samantha caught the shoulder squeeze he gave Elizabeth.

"She's full of questions."

His hand dropped. "Exactly what we hoped for."

Elizabeth's eyes locked onto Doctor Sadana's for a brief second before he turned away and walked out of the door.

Her nurse arched an eyebrow. "Not what you think, my dear. Now how about a board game to pass the time?"

Her mother came into the room with a bouquet of daisies and kissed Samantha's cheek. "From your dad." She filled a container with water, arranged the blooms, and put them on the window sill. “Look,” she pointed. “Flakes are coming down in a pretty steady stream.”

“No,” Samantha cried out. “What if—”

“Uh-uh.” Elizabeth shot her a look and waggled her finger.

Her mother’s lip pursed slightly “You two holding secrets?”

“We have no secrets, mother.”

“Elizabeth?” Samantha’s mother had a quizzical air about her.

Uh-oh. Here comes the flood of questions.

Samantha pretended to stare out the window.

“Yes, ma’am?”

“Call me Jenny.”

“What’s on your mind Mrs. Brown?” Elizabeth asked, obviously avoiding the informal name.

Her mother frowned before continuing. “Do you have children?”

“I have one child.”

Her mother nodded and put a finger to her chin. “Oh, so you’re married.” She glanced at her hand.

“I’m divorced. If there’s something you’d like to know, you could ask to see my records.”

"Mother," Samantha piped in. "Is this necessary?"

"We haven't chatted, and I'd like to get to know your nurse better."

Elizabeth glanced at her watch. "I can give you another five minutes." She sat on the edge of the bed by Samantha's feet.

"Does your child live with you?"

"Mother," Samantha huffed.

"A few questions. I'm not prying." She crossed her arms over her chest.

"Oh yes you are."

"Maybe we could do this another time. In the cafeteria over coffee," Elizabeth suggested as she stood to go."

Samantha heard a clink. She peeked over the side of the bed.

"My knitting supplies," Elizabeth explained.

"It's a flask." Her mother scooped up and examined the container.

"I can explain," her nurse whispered.

Samantha's mother shook a finger at her. "Just as I thought. I innocently followed you into the bathroom when I arrived, to privately ask you a question. Between your sobs, you guzzled. I saw you through the crack in the stall door."

Elizabeth glanced from one to the other.

"I can't believe you have the job of taking care of my daughter and you're drinking." She unscrewed the lid and whiffed. "What is this smell?"

"If you'd only allow me to give an explanation."

"We can discuss this in front of your supervisor."

"Please stop. I don't want Elizabeth to leave. She's the only one in this hospital I trust."

Elizabeth held Samantha's hand, rubbing her palm vigorously. "Please, she cannot be stressed. We need to take this discussion out of this room immediately."

"Mother, please. You and daddy always told me never to judge before understanding the issue at hand. And you're doing just that. Judging her."

Samantha pressed a hand to her chest where her heart seemed to be pounding harder than usual. Elizabeth jumped to attention.

"Calm down, my dear." She took the stethoscope from around her neck, put the ear tips in, manipulated the tubing, and adjusted the tunable diaphragm.

Samantha's mother stepped around to the other side of the bed. "Is she okay?"

"Mrs. Brown, could you please leave the room? I need to call Doctor Sadana."

"We're not finished here, you know?"

She shivered at her mother's harsh tone and cold gaze.

Elizabeth pointed toward the door. "Please."

Her mother left through the open door.

"My temples are throbbing," Samantha stated. She squeezed her eyes shut.

"You'll be fine, my dear. It's been a stressful time for you and your parents. The wait can be a grueling and an emotional challenge for all concerned."

Samantha rubbed her temples. "My mother usually quizzes everyone she meets."

"She's just protecting you."

Samantha nodded.

"I tend to be that way with my son too. I lost one son years ago and I'm forever shielding the one I have left in my life."

"My heart fluttered when mother yelled at you. I got scared."

"Did you feel pain during our moment of discussion?"

"No. Concern maybe. For you." She reached out her hand and clasped Elizabeth's. "I know you're a good person. That's all that matters to me."

Samantha stared into the depths of her nurse's eyes.

Elizabeth heaved a sigh. “I have my story and I am guilty of trying to conceal my pain in ways unknown to others. I love deeply. Always have, always will and for that I will not excuse myself.”

“So, are we good?” Samantha pulled her blanket up.

“Yes, my dear.”

“I’ll go out and have another chat with your mother.”

“And I’ll Skype my friend.”

The wind howled. Samantha pulled the blanket to her chin.

Please let this storm come and go quickly.

FEBRUARY 13

Monday

Weather forecasters reported the storm that hadn't moved in on Sunday was now on its way, full force. Snow would start piling by nightfall. The temperature had dropped to the teens. Gray clouds darkened and a strong wind arose to swirl the already accumulated snow. Sonic chased some of the crystalline flakes before running back into the warmth of the kitchen.

Jason had prepared a cup of mint tea for his mom and watched while she dallied and sipped.

"Do you have to go in today?" He wrung a dishtowel nervously as some serious thoughts flooded his mind.

I have to tell her before she leaves.

"I do. I have a young patient who's depending on me to distract her."

"From what?"

"An overbearing mother." His mom's piercing stare caught and held his. "Don't say it."

"You're the opposite, though a little overly protective." He reflected for a moment. "The storm is supposed to get bad by evening. You *are* coming back after work, right?"

"Yes, I'll be back though my shift will finish later than usual. Why do you ask?"

Because you sometimes stop along the way and refill your flask tank. Because the roads could be slippery.

"Tomorrow's your big day." She continued without waiting for his answer. "Grandma and I have a surprise for you."

Jason started to pace.

How am I going to tell her?

"Is anything wrong, Jase?"

He needed to get this talk over with before his mom went to work, but lacked the balls to even start the conversation.

"Come on. You can level with me. I won't get mad." She laughed. "Did you speed on your skateboard and a policeman ticketed you?"

Jason didn't answer.

She pounded the table and giggled. "I know. You brought a female into your bedroom."

Jason knew what he had to say, even though his mouth stuck like glue, holding his lips closed.

"I know you sometimes smoke."

Her expression didn't show any signs of shock about smoking, which surprised him.

I wish my topic was that easy.

His mom's smile dissolved. Her back stiffened. She intertwined her fingers. When her gaze lifted, the light faded from her hazel eyes until they turned dark and empty.

Shit.

Jason became the bunny and she the tiger. She would pounce at any moment. She would devour him with anger when she realized what he'd done behind her back.

"It's about your dad, isn't it?"

His head moved slowly up and down.

"Don't tell me he and that bimbo are coming to Colorado."

"Dad's coming alone."

"I don't believe you. He wouldn't drive all the way here to see you, or even his own mother, by himself."

"Darla promised."

"And you believe that hussy? The one who fricking screwed my husband while we lived together and made him break his vows?"

"She said she didn't—"

His mom jumped up from the chair and looked him up and down. She put a finger to his chest and pushed. "Conniving. Just like your dad."

Dark pools of fear clouded her eyes.

She's scared she'll lose me too.

"You want to see you dad, go ahead. Just not in this house."

"He's coming for my birthday and he wants to fix our relationship."

"You spoke to him? He mentioned the word *fix*?"

"Well, not exactly."

Her voice lowered to a whisper. "Are you telling me *she*, the one who's living with him in sin, is working all this out for you?"

His eyes moistened.

Damn tears stay put.

What he had to say next would blow his mother's mind. At this point Jason had no choice. He had to tell her the rest.

"They got married."

The blood drained from her face. Her fists tightened. She blinked and peered sightlessly at the wall.

"I'm sorry, mom. I want things the way they used to be, just like you." He winced. "It's too late for the past to rewind."

She didn't speak or look at him. Her immobile stare remained at the nothing land behind him.

"Mom, please. Talk to me."

When she turned her gaze to his, she squinted and brought her hand over her eyes, shielding them as if the sun were too bright. She eyed him with disbelief. "You don't know how a broken heart feels. One day you'll reflect on this moment and know how the kick in the stomach you just gave me hurts like hell."

"He's got a present for me." Jason grasped at any topic. "You could have dinner with us."

She shook her head forcefully. "Count me out, Jason. I will not see him while he's here."

"It's not my fault you two couldn't get along. Fricking hell you both caused me." He'd never raised his voice to his mom.

Her body jerked to attention.

"My shift ends at seven. When I get home, there had better not be a single sign he stepped one foot in this house." She took a deep breath. Her hands trembled. "And forget the evening celebration your grandma and I had planned."

"Mom, please don't be mad. I just need to resolve some things with dad."

"Next, you'll be telling me you're moving to California."

"You know better than that. I wouldn't leave you or grandma."

Her vision narrowed once more. She walked to the front door, picked up her coat and day bag, then walked out the door without saying goodbye.

Jason's chest hurt. His mom used to tell him to never go to bed mad and she'd just left madder than hell.

He went into his room, opened the desk drawer, and grabbed the bottle of Fentanyl. He shook the container wildly in his hand.

Enough to either die or have a good high.

Words ran through his brain.

Alcoholism, addiction, unfaithfulness. Damn them all.

"Am I any better than my parents if I give in to the pain I'm feeling right now?" His own voice sounded raspy, unrecognizable.

He walked slowly to the bathroom with the container in his hand. Chances are the whole bottle would overdose and then kill him. Could he eliminate his agony playing the blood and guts games in real life? Would his pain ever completely go away? What would become of his mom if he left? His grandma?

He opened the door. The commode stood in front of him, the sink to the left.

And Sam?

The word *fate* struck him like a bull running into a red brick wall. Jason pushed down on the container lid with his hand and turned. He emptied the pills in his palm. His eyes blurred, clouded over with tears.

I've lost my bearings in a cloud of fog. Need to get my direction back on the right path.

"Those words came from somewhere. I didn't say them." He looked to the ceiling.

Grandpa?

He turned to the toilet, threw all the pills into the water, and flushed.

"Why the shit did I just toss those down the drain?"

Unrecognizable words churned around his mind. Maybe too many computer blood and gut games had burned up his brain.

Okay now. Take care of Sam.

He went back into his room to sit behind his computer. He clicked on #heartmatch.

Please be there.

She wasn't.

He Skyped. No answer.

What if something happened to her? I'd never know.

He grabbed his phone, hit contacts, found her number and pressed Facetime.

She picked up on the second ring. He almost lost it. The pit of his stomach felt like a wrench gripping a bolt and turning.

“Hey,” he breathed a sigh of relief.

“Hey yourself.”

“You busy?”

“No.”

Her hair flowed around her shoulders. He’d never seen such red-gold abundance before.

“Sam, I have a present I want to mail to you,” he lied. “Can you tell me which hospital you’re in?”

“Ah, such a nice thought.”

“And?”

“Promise you won’t try to come to see me?”

“I promise.” Fingers crossed. “I’ll send your gift out today.”

“Okay.”

“Can we meet up later though?”

“You mean when it’s all over?” She didn’t smile and lowered her chin.

Jason hadn’t done so well in responding to his mom earlier on. He needed to say the right thing now.

“Sam, look at me.”

Her gaze lifted.

"If I could give you my heart, I would." He tried smiling. She didn't respond. "I've done some research and we're probably not a blood type match, so—"

"So?" She asked.

"I want you to know that you have a part of my heart anyway."

Her expression seemed uncertain. "I don't understand."

"I—I like you a lot." He'd never told a girl his inner thoughts before and meant it. At nineteen maybe he'd just ruined his chances with this angel who'd come to mind every time he connected or disconnected from his computer.

A frown flitted across her brow. "I'm sick. I might die." She rubbed her eyes like she'd cry.

"That's not possible."

"What makes you say that?"

"Because—" he took in a deep breath and expelled the air out slowly. "Because fate brought us together, so you couldn't die."

"I don't get what you're telling me."

He shrugged. "I don't know, Sam. Maybe we just have to wait and see what destiny's plan is."

Her dark expression went from thoughtful to radiant, her eyes shining a bright blue.

The color of the sky on a perfect day.

"But we met online."

"I'm saying that didn't happen by coincidence."

"You said before—"

"I know. I know. Well, I made a mistake. Fate is real."

The corners of her mouth lifted.

"When I hang up, text me the address of your hospital and I'll send something nice over for you. A Valentine's Day present."

Her lips parted, showing the most perfect teeth.

Jason put a finger to her smile.

"That's my girl."

He hung up and minutes later the address came through.

Shit. The same hospital where my mom works.

"Well, thank God *they'll* never meet."

Jason knew exactly what he wanted to get. He glanced outside as he got dressed. The snow had picked up. If he couldn't ride his skateboard, he'd jog to buy what he wanted. A warm jacket and tennis shoes came next.

"I'll take the present to Sam myself. Tomorrow." He grinned and glanced at the ceiling.

Grandpa, you stay out of this.

A couple of puffs on a joint and out the door he flew.

###

That's my girl.

She smiled. Her dad said that to her and now Jason.

Nurse Elizabeth entered.

"Nice to see you smiling." She glanced around the room. "Your mother's not here?

Samantha shook her head. "Mother wanted to get home before dark. Is everything okay between you two?"

"We had our discussion and now we understand each other."

"Will she tell on you?"

Elizabeth stopped dead still and her body wilted. Samantha's question had taken Elizabeth aback.

"I'll stay while you're in the hospital. Don't worry Samantha," she patted her hand. "Could I ask what brought about this pleased appearance that fills the room with brightness?"

"A guy I met online."

"Sometimes computer technology isn't always a positive. You're sure he's not a predator in disguise?"

"We've Skyped and Facetimed. I'll put my trust in him as I have in you."

"I'm so glad to see your spirits have lifted."

"I just want my daddy here. I can't be truly relaxed until he's right here beside me."

"He'll be here soon, right?" Elizabeth commented as she walked to the window to peek out.

"Yes. Tomorrow."

Elizabeth shivered. "It's sure cold and blowing right now."

Samantha focused on the window. She wondered if Jason had a car.

"I've got a long twelve-hour shift to do tomorrow."

Samantha turned with a questioning stare.

"When the weather's bad, we take on longer shifts so some of the nurses who live further away can stay home."

"Isn't the bad weather supposed to stop today?"

"The forecasters have lengthened their prediction. The storm will carry through a few more days."

"No," Samantha moaned and picked up her cell phone. She let the phone ring five times before her dad's voicemail picked up. She left a message.

"Daddy?" She covered part of her phone and watched Elizabeth change the TV channel. "Call me."

Elizabeth lowered the volume before pointing to the weather channel. "That's the lingering storm, right there in red."

Samantha blinked several times as tears threatened to fall. "Isn't the weather better above the clouds?"

"Probably," Elizabeth answered. She hurried over to the window to peer out once again. "The snow is blowing sideways." Glancing at her watch and then the television again, she sighed loudly.

"Are you driving home?"

"I have to. My son would become frantic if I stayed here all night." She gave Samantha the bright-eyed look of an optimist, then winked. "I had chains put on at noontime, so I'll be fine. And then back in the morning before you know it."

Samantha nodded as other thoughts besides her dad's trip raced through her mind. "In one of the pamphlets I read, a paragraph said the donor has to be a blood match, right?" She didn't wait for an answer. "What blood type am I?"

"O Positive."

"Does that hurt my chances?"

Elizabeth shook her head. “It’s the most common and so it’s the most frequently matched. We’ll be just fine when the time comes.”

“Heart size counts too.” Samantha said insistently.

“That’s a critical factor.” Elizabeth grew pensive. “You’ve been briefed. You know the answers already, so what’s up with the questions?”

“My online friend said he’d give me his heart if he could.” Samantha reflected momentarily. “Then he said he probably wouldn’t be a match anyway.”

Elizabeth’s brow arched. “Now that’s what I call a true friend.”

“He’s sending me a present.”

“In this weather?” Elizabeth smiled. “He must be driving a truck.”

“Oh, he’s not coming over. He’ll send my package by special delivery.”

“How can he resist a quick once-over of such a beautiful girl on Valentine’s Day?”

“He promised he wouldn’t try to visit me.” She dialed her dad again.

Her dad’s face popped into the phone frame.

“Hey, precious. Sorry I missed your last call.”

“Daddy are you still coming?”

"Our personal newsman said the storm had strengthened, so last night—"

"No" Samantha cried out. "You're not going to make the trip?"

"I'll be there, my love. I called your mother and told her all about the next part of my journey. I asked her to stay put at home. Driving in Denver is hazardous right now."

"When, daddy? When will you get here?"

"Hey, slow down. We left yesterday by plane and landed in Utah. I'll leave tomorrow after a good night's sleep."

"Couldn't an airplane lose control below the clouds?"

"I rented a car and I'll drive from here to Wyoming and then on the highway south to you. Maybe there'll be some wind between the borders, though the highway should be clear of snow by then."

"What if—"

Elizabeth stroked her arm.

"Hello, Elizabeth." Samantha's dad said. "We didn't talk the last time I saw you."

Elizabeth waved.

"Are you staying the night at the hospital?"

Elizabeth shook her head.

"She has to get back to her son or he'll get upset."

Her dad smiled and then put a finger to the screen. “Sleep well tonight, Sammy. I’ll call you along the way on my drive. I love you, sweetheart.”

“Me too, daddy.”

Her dad broke the connection.

“You see, he’s more than halfway here,” Elizabeth said. “Now a few more things to do here and after that, I’ll tuck you in and head home.”

“I probably won’t sleep. I’m so excited about tomorrow.”

“Don’t over-exert yourself with anxiousness though. Keep your mind free from thought tonight.”

“I’ll try.”

Elizabeth turned off the television and checked her vitals. She changed the IV as Samantha put her earplugs in and plugged them into her phone.

Music. Loud music.

The only way she could sleep.

###

The television gave background noise. “Storm worsening. Airport crews can’t keep up with falling snow.”

“Hearts *can* be fixed,” Jason muttered to himself as he held Samantha’s gift. “This will prove something to her.”

He pulled out his phone. Darla had left a message and her phone number. *"I just might have a birthday present for you too."*

He pressed *call back*. After a number of unanswered rings, he hung up. The evening before, he'd spoken to Darla on Skype and knew his dad's plans for leaving Los Angeles for Denver.

I could call him but I'm still mad. When he gets here he'd better apologize or I'm not talking to him.

Jason tried Skyping Darla. She didn't answer.

He pressed contacts on his phone and tried her cell number again. He got her voicemail after the tenth ring.

"Hi, it's Jason. Just wanted to tell you I think you're downright sick. Talk soon."

Jason hung up.

A betrayal to mom? She never has to know.

He glanced at the TV. "Denver is the epicenter of the storm. Tomorrow, on the day of hearts, many roads might be closed.

He let Sonic out and stayed by the door until his best buddy ran back in, then moved back to his bedroom.

The front door slammed. His mother stomped her boots. Jason's door stood open. He waited. His mom walked past his doorway, down the hall, and into her room. Jason strode across the room and kicked the door shut.

She's still mad about dad coming tomorrow. Well, let her sleep on it.

Sonic whined.

Go to her.

That voice again.

"In the morning," he whispered to himself. "I'll surprise her with breakfast and ask for a ride to the hospital." He grinned at that idea.

Jason sat down behind his computer and turned on the games. For tonight, he'd fight the enemy and win.

FEBRUARY 14

Tuesday

Jason stared at the ceiling.

That damned dream. So realistic.

A menagerie of people had surrounded him. Some he knew and some he didn't. His grandpa, his mom, Sonic—they'd all been there. Jason reached to pet his furry friend lying next to him on the bed. Everyone had tried to warn him about something. Their arms had stretched out and for the life of him, he hadn't been able to escape. He glanced at the nightstand clock.

Can't be. Holy crap.

He clicked the television remote, realized his clock had the correct time, and jumped out of bed. He raced through the doorway to his mom's room.

Mom's not here?

He listened for the sounds of his mom in the kitchen.

Unusually quiet.

The hairs on the back of his neck stood straight up. He didn't know why. At the end of the hallway he glanced at the coatrack.

Fake fur coat and day bag gone.

Sonic followed him to the front door. He opened it and looked out for her car. He could barely see. Snow whipped sideways. Cold hammered against his bare chest. The driveway had two inches of fresh snow with drifts on both sides. Tire tracks led into the street.

"Mom shoveled and left. No good-byes?"

Sonic lifted a leg on the snowy porch column to pee.

Jason shivered from both the wintry chill and from worry. "Maybe she left a note on the table."

He closed the door and strode quickly through the living room to the kitchen. Relief passed through him as he noticed the sheet of yellow paper on the tablecloth. He read.

Hunker down today. The snow is drifting. Only emergency crews and medical personal are supposed go out in this blizzard. I'll text you as I'm leaving the hospital after my shift is over. I love you Jase. Sorry for not telling you last night. Stay warm. Love you always, Mom.

He walked to the fridge with a satisfied grin on his face.

Alone for the day.

His grandma wouldn't chance going out in weather like this. He prepared a grilled cheese, chips, and a soda for breakfast.

Too early to Facetime Sam.

Jason ate, showered, dressed, smoked a joint, and sat down by his computer to play some games.

He tried Darla's number again. He left a message on her voicemail. "Hey, it's me, Jason. Call me back when you can."

The TV continued to repeat and update storm news. "Rocky Mountain drivers are sliding across the city. The worst whiteout in years."

Jason briefly wondered if his dad had gotten caught in the storm. He'd driven tanks through desert sand storms during his military stint.

A little blizzard wouldn't phase him.

After a trip to the hospital to visit Sam and say hello to mom, he'd return home before his dad stopped by and picked him up for dinner. Both his mom and Sam would have a nice shock when he showed up. And his dad? While he was looking forward to seeing him, well, he'd better come up with some good answers before Jason would even begin to forgive him for leaving.

Sonic jumped on the bed and snuggled into the covers. Jason pulled up a new game, homed in on the characters, gave them machine guns, and began the chase.

###

Elizabeth held Samantha's hand as she watched the weather channel. Lunch came and went and still no news from her dad. Her mom had stayed home.

Samantha stared at the television. According to the news, drivers were out there, trudging down the roadways. Airports cancelled flights and many travelers had become stranded. A foot of blowing snow would completely efface the major thoroughfares before nightfall.

"Let's turn off the television," Elizabeth suggested.

Samantha shook her head.

"Okay. Then I'll turn it down."

A quick glance at her cellphone, nestled on top of the covers, showed no messages from either her dad or Jason.

Where is everyone?

Snow covered the window. Her mother phoned, trying to reassure Samantha that her dad had probably stopped for lunch along the way.

She dialed Jason. He picked up on the second ring. Samantha wanted to cry.

"Hey." The words clogged somewhere in her throat.

"Hi, Sam. Happy Valentine's Day."

She nodded.

"You there?"

"Like I'd move," Samantha answered.

Jason chuckled. "Your gift should arrive soon."

Samantha watched as Elizabeth stepped out of the room. "Happy Birthday Jason," she uttered shyly.

"I'm going to freeze a slice of cake for you." He chuckled. "If there's any left after tonight. I'm waiting for my dad to pick me up and he used to love chocolate cake. He's coming in sometime soon and taking me to dinner."

"He can still drive on the roads?"

"My dad? Yeah, he'll make it. What about yours?"

"He's not answering his phone. I'm so worried."

"Don't worry, Sam. He's probably trying to find a store to buy a bouquet of flowers."

"He could get flowers on the ground floor of the hospital. What if he's had a wreck somewhere?"

"Think positive. You'll see him soon and realize you worried for nothing."

"Are you watching television?"

"Yep. Remember my mom has to drive in this storm when she gets off work."

Samantha pointed. "Look at the TV, Jason. Stretches of highways are closing. And—" she hesitated.

Elizabeth came in and turned off the TV. Samantha's phone screen went blank at that precise moment.

"My dear. I'll be back soon. I need to make an emergency run. Call your mom and talk to her while I'm gone."

"Don't leave me," Samantha cried. "I'm so scared."

"Nothing to be afraid of." Elizabeth hugged her. "I'll be right back."

Another nurse came into the room and nodded to Elizabeth.

"This is Becky, sweetie. She'll stay with you until I get back."

"But—"

Elizabeth hurried away.

###

"Damn phone." Jason couldn't find his charger.

He kept one eye on the TV news channel.

Denver highways impassible. Bus and light rail suspended. All flights cancelled. Passengers stuck. Because of a major crash, one hundred cars stranded on highways leading in and out of Denver. Ambulances trying to get through.

At that moment, Jason found his phone charger and plugged in. A message from his mom popped up.

"Leaving the hospital. I'll call."

"Shit. She sent that text thirty minutes ago."

He looked up from his phone to the TV screen. Back to his phone and once again to the news report. Jason fell to his knees. His phone dropped to the floor.

Mom's in that accident. I just know it.

And he vomited.

###

A snow plow, Jason. Git movin'.

Jason shook his head to clear the cobwebs and got to his elbows.

Why do I upchuck every time I'm fricking panicked?

He got to his knees.

More crap to clean up before mom—.

Jason jumped to his feet. "Mom. Accident. Get the fricking hell on the road to the hospital." He cursed because he had to waste time cleaning up the vomit with a wet face towel before he left the house.

He grabbed gloves, wrapped himself into his warm ski jacket, slipped into boots, and opened the front door. The cold, sharp air took his breath away. He took his ski cap out of the insulated pocket of his coat and slid the mask over his head.

Jason couldn't see where the steps were supposed to be. He jumped and landed perfectly on a thick patch of snow where the sidewalk should be. A snow plow sat idle at the end of his driveway. Getting to the driveway with all the blinding, face-freezing snow and fierce winds proved to be a challenge. Jason slid down the icy path to the plow and climbed in.

"It's running," he muttered to himself. "Get the hell out of here before the driver dude comes back."

Drive this machine like grandpa's tractor.

He tried shifting. Nothing moved.

Damn. This is nothing like any farm machine.

"Hey, Bud. What you doin' with my vehicle here?"

Don't turn. Act like you don't hear him.

Jason didn't know how to drive this huge piece of equipment and he had to get to the hospital.

"Trying to get to the hospital. My mom's been in an accident."

"You sure about that, Dude?"

"Yes," Jason whispered. "I need to get there fast."

"Scoot over, Dude. I'll get you there."

Jason nodded and almost cried with relief. "Can you stop calling me Dude?"

"Will do. Now which hospital we goin' to?"

###

Doctor Sadana appeared at her bedside.

"Samantha, I have good news for you."

She turned. Her eyes welled with tears. "The highways are closing. My dad's somewhere out there and—"

"My dear. We've sent for your mother. We have a donor heart match." He turned to the nurse. "Nurse Becky will prepare you and wheel you down to surgery."

"No one's here with me. I'm so scared."

"The police are bringing your mother over immediately," Doctor Sadana advised.

"No," she cried. "I want my daddy." Hot tears ran down her face and long hiccupping sobs robbed her of breath.

"Samantha, calm down. You cannot get so excited. Your heart—"

She started panting and lowered her voice to a whisper. "I will not go with you without my dad."

"That could be too late. The heart must be implanted quickly," Doctor Sadana reached for her arm.

Samantha jerked away. "Don't touch me." Her body shook as a low moan, resembling that of a wounded animal, resounded over the walls.

"I'm here, Sam."

She looked up as Jason walked into the room and hurried over to her bed.

Suddenly quiet filled the room.

Samantha looked at Jason. "You're here. I asked you not to come."

"Fate brought me here." He pulled out the clumsily wrapped package. "Happy Valentine's Day."

Samantha opened the present. A silver heart on a chain. "It's a broken heart."

"It can be fixed. Place the jagged pieces together," Jason encouraged.

She did.

"Turn the whole heart over now."

"It's inscribed. It says, *'Fate brought us together.'*"

"You'll wear one half and I," Jason pulled out a matching chain, "will take the other half."

Samantha didn't say anything.

"I'm here for you, Sam. I won't move until this doctor," he glanced at Doctor Sadana, "tells me your new heart is beating." He took in a deep breath. "I'll wait for your parents too."

"And Nurse Elizabeth?"

Jason frowned thoughtfully and then smiled.

"Nurse Elizabeth," he nodded. "Yes, I'll wait for my mom right here in this spot too."

Samantha gasped. "She's your mother?"

"Unless there are two nurses on this floor named Elizabeth, I would imagine that's her."

Doctor Sadana nodded. "It's her alright. You must be Jason."

"Yep."

"Samantha, we need to get you prepared now. Sorry Jason, you'll have to wait in the waiting room."

"Will you be here when I wake up?" Samantha asked.

"I will stay here forever if I have to."

Doctor Sadana nodded to Nurse Becky. "Get her ready. I'll have the gurney sent in. Samantha," he clasped her hand. "I'll be with you until I turn you over to this young man right here."

Samantha nodded.

He laid a hand on Jason's shoulder. "Tell this beautiful young lady you'll meet her in recovery and then you need to leave so we can get busy."

“Thank you for the gift Jason. I’m sorry I couldn’t get you a birthday present.”

“You are my birthday present. I’ll be waiting.” He pointed. “Somewhere out there.”

He turned to leave.

“Jason? Will one heart work for us?” She held up the necklace.

“You’d better believe it.” And he left the room.

EPILOGUE

April

An abundance of tall weeds from a nearby field waved with the gentle breeze. Birds chirped on budding branches and squirrels scampered across the bright green blades of grass poking through the earth. A cloudless blue sky spread from the plains to the mountain tops.

Samantha lay extended on the colorful quilt depicting pictures from her life, at least up to this point. Her strawberry-blond locks had been braided and hung over her left shoulder. She wore a white scooped-neck T-shirt and loose navy-blue sweats. The sandals she had toed off lay to the side of the coverlet.

"Here. Put this under your head." Jason beat the pillow he'd found in the trunk on his knee before placing it under her lifted head.

Samantha inhaled. "The air has an aromatic freshness. Thank you for driving me here today, Jason."

He sat down beside her and pointed to the silver band on her wrist. “How long do you have to wear the ID?”

“My transplant alert bracelet?” Samantha shrugged. “Everything from now on is about timing. When I take my medications. When I go in for blood work. When I have another biopsy.” She stared at the sky. “And going back to school in the fall.”

“School’s a good thing, right?”

“It’s necessary for me to mingle again, or so my mother says.”

He chuckled.

“What’s so funny?”

“You.” Jason ran a knuckle down her cheek. “Your dad wanted to come with us on your first venture away from home. You should have seen your expression.”

“He just took another month off work. Daddy thinks I can’t do anything by myself.”

“He cares and is doing just what all dads would do with a child in your situation.” Jason thought for a moment. “We had some good chats while you recuperated in the hospital. He’s a good man.”

Samantha smiled. “And my mother?”

“I think she’s beginning to like me.”

She cupped her hand to whisper. “They’re driving me crazy with attention. Mom even wants to wipe me when I go to the toilet.”

“Sam, you’re lucky to have them and—"

“Yeah, I get their concern. You never know when something could happen to those you love.”

Jason nodded. “We saw the unexpected during the February blizzard.” He snapped his fingers. “Poof. A life came and went just like that.”

“Tell me the story again. The one where everyone went crazy in the hospital waiting room.”

“Well, once upon a time—”

“No, silly. The real story of what happened on Valentine’s Day.”

“Again?”

She nodded.

“You should know it by heart,” he took in a deep breath before continuing. “I’ve told you that tale over and over. Surely you’ve memorized it by now.”

She pouted. “Your deep voice is mesmerizing. Please?”

“I’ll record that frightful night on my phone and send it to you,” he laughed.

“One more time and I’ll never ask again,” she pleaded.

Samantha put a hand over her eyes to shade the sun. Jason cleared his throat before beginning.

“Your rolling stretcher—”

“Gurney,” Samantha corrected.”

“Hey. Who’s telling this? You or me?”

Samantha giggled. She nibbled her bottom lip and gave the zip up sign in front of her mouth.

“Your gurney headed down the hallway out of sight that day and I went the other direction to the waiting room. At first, I sat alone for the longest time. I got a soda and candy bar from the machine and watched the news about the snowstorm. The roads had closed and the police told everyone not to venture outside.”

Samantha’s eyes widened. She knew what came next.

“Your mother came flying in through the double doors. She stopped, putting a hand to her chest and asked where you were. I told her they’d already taken you into surgery. She fell into an armchair.”

“She cried, right? My mother seems so rigid sometimes but let something happen to me and her emotions break like a dam does in flood waters.”

“I consoled her until suddenly my mom came rushing in through those same doors.”

"Did you bawl then too?"

Jason shook his head. "My temples pounded like crazy though because I thought she had been in the accident I saw on TV. In truth she had been called away to help with the victims in the highway crash."

"Did my mother and your mom have words for each other?"

"No. My mom told your mother to stay seated and behave herself until further notice. She told me she was assisting with your surgery and left the room."

"My dad must have come in about then."

"Yep. He hurried in all wet with snow. His car had gone into a ditch and the police brought him to the hospital. He'd hoped to see you before surgery. He got upset after learning he wouldn't be able to tell you he loved you."

Samantha turned on her side. "I want to sit up."

Jason gave her a long, surprised look and then offered his hand.

"I can manage by myself, although I love it when you take both of my hands to help me."

Jason smiled. "Anything to please my Princess. Here's some water. Keep hydrated, remember?"

Samantha drank. "Go on."

“My dad flew into the room next. He entered crying hysterically. I couldn’t understand him. Actually, your mother calmed him down.”

“And up to that point, they didn’t know each other.”

“Right.” Jason ran a finger down Samantha’s arm. “I’d never seen him so emotional.”

“When did you find out about Darla?”

“Right then. I thought my dad would drive alone to Colorado. Darla had told me she would stay in California.”

“She tricked him?”

“Yep. She’d got behind the seventh seat of his SUV and stayed hidden until he stopped to rest at a motel along the way.”

“Then she showed up at his door?”

“Yep. She entered his hotel room and by then dad had no choice. He had to bring her along on the rest of the trip.”

Jason took in a deep breath.

“As dad entered Denver, someone slid out of control, hitting the passenger side of his vehicle. His car spun around heading the other direction, causing a chain reaction. So many cars were involved. The rescue workers said my dad was lucky to be alive. People and rammed vehicles were all over the highway. Some were injured, some dazed and—” he shivered, “and a few dead or dying.”

"The next part is so sad."

"The EMT got Darla out and rushed her to the hospital. They put her on life support, but she didn't make it. None of us in the waiting room knew that she had died, and we didn't know she'd be a perfect match and your donor heart."

"You liked her, didn't you?"

"She wanted me to make up with my dad. She encouraged me to go to college and to stop smoking joints." He thought for a moment. "She seemed sincere."

"And she truly loved your dad."

"I think they loved each other."

"Fate had a different plan." Tears welled on Samantha's lashes.

Jason nodded. He lifted a finger to go from the top of her scar, down the front of her shirt, following the invisible line to the bottom where his finger stopped.

"You're here today because of Darla."

"I'm sorry for her mom and sister."

"Dad says her mom wants to meet you one day."

"I'd like that—one day." Samantha swiped at tears running down her cheeks. "So, end of story?"

"Uh-uh. No way. Not for us at least."

"We've all changed in our own way." Sonic plopped down beside her. Samantha rested a hand on his back to scratch between his shoulder blades.

"I had to get a job if I wanted my own place. I'll sling burgers to pay the rent for a while."

"Can you take me to your apartment sometime?" Samantha seemed pensive. "Do you miss living with your mom and seeing your grandma every day?"

"Yes, and yes," he laughed. "My dad has moved back in with mom and they're talking things over. It's better I'm not around. Kind of embarrassing. I mean are they fricking sleeping together or what? And besides I'm not sure their story could ever start over."

"Maybe it could. Don't judge them."

"My mom stopped drinking." He sighed. "She's attending meetings."

Samantha took Jason's hand. "You're going to college in the fall?"

"Yep. I'll start out local and then I'll see where I'm headed."

"Are you still into your online games?"

"Not much anymore. I used the games to vent when my dad and I stopped talking."

###

"I like your new look, Jason. Did you dress up for me?"

"Thrift shop goodies," he grinned.

Samantha ran a finger down his chin. He smiled as he remembered the first thing she'd said when she woke up from surgery.

Jason, you waited for me.

Jason lifted his gaze to the sky. "No spring showers. At least for today."

Samantha moved closer to him. Jason lowered his head and lightly kissed her. She acted surprised.

"You pulled away. Are you scared about kissing me? Afraid my healing heart will pound too fast?"

"Well, sort of."

"Jason, you can't hurt me." Samantha put a hand to the back of his head and pulled him in.

Her tongue searched for and found his. She moved her mouth inches away and whispered. "Now that's the way I like to be kissed. Just remember that for the next time."

"And when will that be?"

Samantha removed the heart necklace from her pocket. "When I can wear this around my neck again. When I can drive. And most of all, when we're alone together. Totally," she glanced around, "and completely alone."

"Idea Sam."

"What's that?"

"Let's take a selfie. We need to get a fresh start on a new blanket for grandma Rosie to make." Jason pulled out his phone, moved in close to Samantha and clicked several pictures.

They kissed and Jason clicked again. They hugged. Another click.

"Thank you, Jason. You stayed with me throughout my surgery, during the days in intensive care, after that in the hospital room, and at my home. I don't know if I'll ever be able to thank you enough. I survived because of you."

"You're here because of fate. You taught me that life isn't about coincidence. Made me believe in myself and that anything could be possible."

"I longed for life and now I have a new beginning."

"I think we both have a new start."

Sonic moved into the perimeter. Jason snapped another picture.

He smiled. "Now, it's to get you home before your dad comes looking for us." He picked Samantha up.

"I can walk," she insisted.

"Just this once, let me hold you tight."

She wrapped her arms around his neck. Sonic ran ahead to the old jalopy Jason drove and started barking.

"What the heck," Jason muttered.

"He's barking at a box. Put me down. Just hold my hand and walk with me."

As they got closer to Jason's car, Sonic went wild, turning around and around in circles.

Jason peeked in. "It's a scraggly black puppy."

"Did someone purposely put him there?"

"I bet he's been dumped. Kinda like when I found Sonic."

"We can't just leave him," Samantha pleaded.

Jason grinned. "I'd never leave an animal, just like I didn't leave you."

"Are you sayin' I'm an animal?"

"After that last kiss, I hope so." He lifted the puppy out. "It's a she."

She laughed. "Let's call her *Lucky*. Can you keep her at your place?"

"I'm allowed two animals in my apartment."

"Then that means I can never visit?"

He frowned. "Why?"

"You just called me an animal. That would make three if you count correctly."

Jason laughed and bent down to kiss her. The puppy squealed, so they pulled apart.

"Call your dad and tell him we'll be back in an hour. Let's get some puppy food and get this little gal settled in my apartment."

"Okay and then?" Samantha smiled.

"Your necklace, remember."

She touched her pocket. "I do."

"When you're finally able to wear your half, I'll show you around my quarters. Until then, let's keep our cool.

"You mean like crackalackin?"

Jason chuckled. "Not exactly. You'll learn more slang as time moves along."

"Put the box in the back seat so Lucky won't fall out. Then I want to tell you something."

Jason put Lucky into the back and then closed the door after Sonic jumped in.

"Sup?" Jason grinned.

Samantha leaned against the car and crooked her finger. "Come closer."

He stood in front of her. She clutched his T-shirt and pulled him into her body, wrapped her arms around him, and then kissed him for a long time. When Jason stepped back he searched her eyes.

"Can we make it, Jason?"

"What are you askin' me?"

"Are we short-term or long-term?"

Jason put his hands on her shoulders. "We take everything a day at a time. No plans. Just today and then when tomorrow comes, we do the same thing."

"Until what?"

"Sam, what's up with all these questions?"

"What if my body rejects my new heart?"

"Isn't there something in this story about what ifs?"

"Yes. Your mom told me not to question. To go day-by-day."

"So, what are you really worried about?"

"Timing. I'm afraid that somewhere, somehow my timing will be off and something will go wrong."

"And that's because all your life has been a struggle, right?"

"I never knew what could happen next. I don't know how not to question everything."

"So, let me teach you." He tilted her chin up and kissed her lips softly. "Let's begin with this."

"What's my lesson?"

"Not to ask questions. Accept this kiss for what it is. A moment of caring. A feeling of love. Let it go at that."

"And tomorrow?"

“You’ll wake up in your own bed, happy to be alive. Feel glad that you have another day.”

“Because someone didn’t get that chance? Like Darla?”

“There you go questioning again. Relax. Don’t put a question mark to everything you’re thinking.”

“That’s easy for you to say.”

“I’ve done the questioning too, Sam. When my dad left. I blamed myself, thinking he’d really gone because I’d made him unhappy.” He inhaled and exhaled slowly. “I learned to live each day as it happens because of you.”

“What—”

“There you go with a question again. Give me a statement. Try it. You’ll catch on.”

He caught her questioning gaze and with his finger lifted her chin. “Try just once for me.”

“Ah, ah,” she stuttered.

“Think about tomorrow morning,” Jason encouraged.

“I’ll wake up being grateful.” She hesitated. “Hug my parents and—”

“Wait for me to pick you up.”

“Yep. I can do that.” She smiled. “And the day after that?”

“One day at a time.”

"Okay." Her shoulders relaxed. Probably for the first time in years. "Let's get Lucky some food and settle her in and then you can drive me home."

"That's my girl. And before I leave your house I'll kiss you again."

"Whoa. In front of my parents?"

"That's a question."

"Okay then. How about—not in front of my parents."

Jason laughed. "You'll get used to not making everything into a what if. That's all we're working on for now."

"Okay. Sounds good."

"Tomorrow we'll take Lucky to the vet to see if she's chipped. If not, we'll get her shots and take her home."

"And after that, you'll kiss me again."

"Hey, you're getting the hang of this conversation."

"A day at a time," she repeated.

They got into the car. Samantha put a hand on his knee.

"In about four months I'll be driving."

Jason turned to gaze at her before he started the car. "And then you'll be drivin' me around." He laughed.

"Yep. You got that one right."

He leaned over to kiss her before he turned the key.

"Let's go to the drive thru and get some burgers before we head to my place. Sonic and Lucky might be hungry."

Samantha nodded. She then placed her hand over her heart and whispered. "Thank you."

Acknowledgements

I would like to thank my editor and cover artist, Lori Corsentino, for her patience and advice along the way.

Please back a local cause, as there are many in our world today. Here are a few of the ones I support:

Learn more about The Gift of Life Donor Program at: www.donors1.org

The research for advanced melanoma.

Help for battered and abused women and children.

Taking care of our Veterans from past and present wars.

Animal shelters. Each volunteer makes an animal smile.

Also by C.K. Alber

C.K. Alber also writes Romantic Suspense. Check out The Promise Series.

Broken Promises

A Promise of Revenge

A Prisoner's Promise

About the Author

C.K. Alber, author of "The Promise Series" and #heartmatch, was born in Indiana and raised and educated in both Indiana and Illinois. An extended move to Europe brought about the desire to write.

She had gone from the maze of corn fields and town life to historical buildings, famous paintings, the city, and the seaside. As a "people watcher" her stories and characters began to develop, her imagination went wild regarding the settings and dialogues in her head, thus, Romantic Suspense, Women's Fiction, and Young Adult became her preferred genres.

Now she lives in Colorado with her beloved, thirteen-year-old rescue dog Luna. She is a dedicated Pescatarian, loves traveling between Washington DC and Colorado to visit family, and is still a worldwide traveler when the occasion arises.